INHERITANCE OF DUST

INHERITANCE OF DUST

MATTHEW RASNAKE

THIS STORY CONTAINS CONTENT WHICH MAY UPSET SOME READERS.

SPECIFIC CONTENT WARNINGS MAY BE FOUND ON THE LAST PAGE.

PROLOGUE

Sol 796, 9 pm
20°0'S 356°35'E
Zubrin Crater, Mars

DUST DEVILS GLIDED ACROSS THE CRATER FLOOR AS THE LAST drop fell into Leana's glass. Luis sat the bottle on the counter, picked up his own glass, and clinked hers in an unspoken toast. They leaned against the counter and sipped their drinks.

"I miss wine," Leana said as she swirled the contents in her glass.

"A few more months," Luis said. "As soon as it's ready, I'll make sure you have some." He set his glass on the counter, wrapped his arms around her, and nestled his face against hers. "Homemade grape juice isn't the same, but let's not forget that this is very special… the first-ever Martian grape juice from the first-ever Martian grapes."

She loved the smell of him, the warmth of his cheek

against hers. Mars may be breathtaking, but after all this time, he could still take hers away.

"True," she said, and smiled.

She treasured these moments—early evening with the children asleep and the day's work complete—when they could finally be together. This was when it felt most like Earth, felt like it had when they'd just started out, just fallen in love—when they'd first planned to be exactly here. The day, the work, and the place fell away, and all that mattered was that they were together.

Tonight felt different, though. After two years with just the four of them here, tonight was the last night they'd be able to say with any confidence that they were the only people awake on the entire planet. Tomorrow, everything would change. Everything they'd worked toward over the last decade would finally begin.

His dream had brought them here, but their love had made it possible. "I couldn't do this without you, you know."

"And I'd be lost without you." He said.

"So true." She flashed him a mischievous smile, and he looked at her in that way she loved. A warm flush rose in her chest and she turned to him, took his glass, and placed it in the sink with her own. "I'll get them in the morning." She took his hand. "Let's go to bed."

PREPARATIONS

Leana wanted to sit down. *Thank God for point-five g's.* She'd finished her final checks on the environmental systems and living units in nineteen separate HABs, and she was beat. It would be nice to have everyone here, finally. At least then she could take a break.

HAB 20's comm system beeped. *"Leana honey,"* Luis said, *"we've got confirmed telemetry from both ships—they're on schedule for landing."*

She loved to hear his voice in an empty HAB—there was something intimate and sexy about the way the computer positioned his voice for her ears, like he was inches from her. "Thanks, sweetheart," she said. "Everything under control there?"

"Oh, yeah. Everybody's where they should be, systems are online, and the lights are shining. It's a beautiful evening, and I can't wait to see those ships land. It's going to be quite a sight! How about you?"

"I'm just wrapping up here," she said, "last one, then I'm going to pick up the kids. We'll be there with the other transport in plenty of time."

"They'll be excited when those ships come in, in…" he paused,

"forty minutes. Pre-entry burns have begun... They're making final trajectory adjustments and getting lined up for their deorbit burns."

"You pay attention to your job," she said, "and we'll see you in about half an hour."

"Yes ma'am!" He said and laughed.

She touched the sTrans patch on her neck as she headed toward the airlock, and said, "Status: Gabriel and Michael Pendrova."

The computer's AI could distinguish commands and requests picked up by the sensor/transceiver patch from general conversation, but she'd never gotten comfortable with the more conversational style of voice interaction that Luis favored. He treated anything with apparent autonomy and a friendly voice interface as part of the crew, but she preferred to maintain a discrete separation and would generally touch the patch to initiate interaction whenever her hands were free enough to do so. It was an affectation that Luis playfully—if somewhat too frequently—needled her over.

Gabriel and Michael Pendrova are coloring in Habitation Pod 1A, Common Room. The computer responded in the casual voice it had evolved for her over the years.

"Thank you," she said, then caught herself and rolled her eyes, glad Luis wasn't there to give her grief. She wasn't completely immune to the AI's personality, and her parents had raised her to be polite by default.

You're welcome.

Leana groaned and imagined Luis' laughter.

She paused at the airlock's inner door and surveyed HAB 20A's common room while she once again ran through her mental checklist of the basic things Tyler and Tamra would need. The HAB looked like a home, if a sparsely decorated one, but they would soon make it their own.

Leana turned and entered the airlock.

"Nanny," she addressed the boys' caretaker AI, "please

have the boys get ready for an excursion. I'll be there in ten minutes."

Of course, Mrs. Pendrova.

Nanny was the one exception she'd made to her arms-length treatment of the algorithms that supported their daily lives. She'd learned early on that it helped the boys when she and Luis treated the AI like a partner and a real person who cared for them. Eventually, they would discover—and likely exploit—Nanny's limitations, but for now they emulated the respect they saw. And it was just easier on her to always treat Nanny the same way.

She latched her helmet in place on her back as she walked toward the airlock between the HAB and the transport. She paused at the threshold as a wave of mild nausea unsteadied her. Instinctively, she checked the suit's dosimeter, which read normal. *Second time today. Good thing the docs are almost here.* She entered the transport and started the automated undock. The airlock doors closed, the centimeters of space between them pressure-cycled, and the seals released. Once clear of the HAB, she took the vehicle's controls and headed toward home.

The transport bounced along the path between HABs, and Mars slid past its south-facing windows—flat and rock-strewn regolith spread out in every direction under the haze of a rust-colored sky. To the north far beyond the HABs, the wall of the crater in which they'd built their little ghost town narrowed until it vanished over the horizon.

Leana hoped she'd never take the view for granted.

The colony's HABs sat in two rows in an arc centered on the large Central Pod, and faced south past the smaller interior crater nearby that they would soon transform into an enormous, domed, green lake. Their home—HAB 1—was nearest to the Central Pod's southwest corner, and only a short drive from HAB 20 on the other side. She engaged the automated docking sequence as she approached.

They would share HAB 1 with Paul and Sheila, their oldest, dearest friends, who—along with her and Luis—were the progenitors of the whole Mars colonization mission.

Leana had taken special care in kitting out the Robinson's B-side common room, decorating it with photo and art reproductions and other items she knew would help them feel at home. She'd even placed seedlings of Sheila's favorite flowers which she'd started with stock from the colony's cryogenic seed vault and nurtured in the greenhouse. Technically, it was an unauthorized use of the vault's seeds, but it would make her friend happy.

And besides, who could've stopped me?

She entered the main airlock and waited while the dust mitigation system's ultrasonic vibrations and air column dislodged and carried away the Martian dust. Once clear, she opened the airlock's inner door to HAB 1's A-side, onto a small landing which overlooked her living room.

There Gabriel darted, naked, around the corner of the couch, up the steps, and down the hallway toward the bedrooms, with Michael—himself only half-dressed—in close pursuit.

"Gabriel!" Michael waved crumpled clothes in the air as he ran. "You have to let me dress you!"

Breathless laughter and a shrill scream were Gabriel's immediate response, followed by, "I can dress me!"

Leana grinned despite herself. "Boys!" Leana said, loudly but calmly, her smile still firmly in place. "Come here, please."

Gabriel ran back into the room, a sock in one hand and a t-shirt in the other, followed closely by Michael.

"I tried Mama, but Gabes wouldn't let me help." Michael said, his gaze fixed on the floor.

"It's all right, Michael," Leana said, "You tried. Gabriel can dress himself, but he's not as quick as you, so you should be patient with him. Now, Gabriel, where are the rest of your clothes?"

Gabriel looked back towards the boy's room.

"Ok. You go get yourself dressed. I'll check on you in two minutes."

"Ok mama," he turned and padded back to his room.

"How about you, Michael?"

"I'm almost ready, Mama," he replied. "Are the other people here?"

"Not yet, but almost," she said. "We're going to go help with the landing, then you two can help me get them to their new homes. Tomorrow we'll meet everyone in the main building to get to know them a little better. You'll get to meet some of the kids tonight, but there won't be much time to play. Our new friends will be very tired."

"I understand."

"Now, please finish getting ready, while I help your brother." Leana held out her hand, which Michael took, and they walked together back towards the bedrooms.

Gabriel was mostly dressed when she entered his small room, though his shirt was on backwards. She helped both of them finish up and, with little argument, herded them back through the living room and into the airlock. The boys grabbed their own pressure suits and helmets from their compartments, and she helped them wriggle in and lock their helmets in place on their backs.

They entered the transport, and she strapped them into their seats, then herself. She disengaged from the airlock and headed for the landing zone.

———

Leana stopped the transport several meters from the one Luis had driven, and waved to him as he turned from his console and waved back. Luis had set up a command console on the ground just outside his transport where the boys, strapped into the back seats, couldn't see him.

"Leana," Luis' voice came over the comm system, "we're about two minutes away from the first deorbit burn."

Behind her, the boys bounced in their seats and shouted, "Daddy, Daddy, Daddy!"

"Alright. Hooking in now." Leana switched her consoles over to the launch and landing dashboards that showed the incoming ships' telemetry and enabled her to patch into comms as needed. "I'm online, switching comms." She set up for two-way with both Luis and Antoniadi One. "Antoniadi One, this is Mars Base. How do you read?"

"Mars Base, Antoniadi One. You're coming in loud and clear, Leana. It's great to hear your voice."

Paul's voice filled her with warmth and hope—had it really been two years since she'd been able to speak to her old friend in anything near real time?

"You too. Now let's get you down here so I can give you a hug."

"You got a deal."

"Mars Base, Antoniadi One."

Sheila! Leana tried not to shout over the comms. "Antoniadi One, go ahead."

"Leana, I suggest you keep your paws off my husband."

Leana laughed. "Oh dear, don't you worry. I've got a hug waiting for you, too."

"Me too, Aunty Sheila!" Michael said, while Gabriel looked down at the transport's floor in silence.

"Oh, and I've got hugs for both you boys," Sheila said, "you just wait till I see you!"

"Clear channel, please," Luis cut in. "Reunions can wait. Deorbit burns in sixty seconds."

The landing zone was the same they'd used when they

arrived nearly two years before, though expanded and significantly improved with the help of the construction rovers. Now two rings of lights defined the cleared and compacted areas where the twin ships would soon set down.

Leana reviewed her displays. "Antoniadi One, Mars Base. Telemetry is looking good."

"Mars Base, we're all greens up here. Deorbit burn in ten."

Luis made a similar call to the sister ship, whose burn would begin sixty seconds after the first.

Indicators flashed as Paul's ship began its burn. Velocity dropped steadily for thirty seconds until Leana's panel lit up with warnings. Numbers continued to flow in, but everything was off program. The ship's velocity had stabilized—apparently all three vacuum engines were out.

Leana grabbed a headset and put it on. "Comms private," she said, "Antoniadi One, Mars Base. What's your status?"

"Having a bit of a bumpier ride up here than we expected, Mars Base. Engines shut down early and so far we haven't been able to bring them back online. We're updating the entry program. We should have plenty of propellant to adjust our entry vector, but we'll be coming in hot."

"Understood," she said. "Stay on top of it. I've got you, Paul."

"No worries here, Mars Base. It'll be fine. Just like the simulations."

Paul was a capable pilot, and both he and the ship could handle much worse. She needn't have worried but for the more than fifty people aboard, including her two best friends.

"Tell the boys we'll see them soon. Antoniadi One, out."

"Will do, Antoniadi One. See you on the ground. Mars Base out."

Leana helped the boys unbuckle and come up to the front to watch the ships land. She and Luis had already discussed the dangers of landing with them, so they were as prepared as they could be. If anything went wrong, she'd talk them through it, and they'd figure out the rest together.

Leana watched the readouts and gave her status report. "Approach and entry vectors are set. Orientation and attitude set. Antoniadi One entry interface in ten seconds. Comms blackout in twenty."

From their vantage point near the landing sites, the ships would appear to rise like shooting stars from the eastern horizon as they compressed the thin Martian atmosphere into a super-heated plasma.

An indicator flashed. "Comms blackout," Leana said. "Receiving good telemetry from satellite passthrough."

Michael was the first to notice the bright flash near the horizon, which grew brighter as it rose. "Mama! Look!" He pointed it out to Gabriel.

"Awaiting voice contact."

The ship left a trail of fire in the sky that dimmed and finally vanished altogether. Leana tried to blink away the afterimage.

"Antoniadi Two entry interface in ten seconds," Luis said.

The comms blackout was expected, but no amount of simulation had prepared Leana for the sick emptiness in her stomach. *C'mon, Paul, let me hear you.* She reviewed the ship's systems in her head as she checked the telemetry again and grasped for reassurance. *We should have heard from him by now.*

A second star rose above the horizon, brighter and higher than the first before it also faded from view.

"Antoniadi Two comms blackout. Telemetry's good from satellite passthrough. Looking good so far," Luis said.

Leana's patience couldn't hold out any longer. "Antoniadi One, Mars base. Standing by."

If they don't make it… She couldn't even finish the thought.

"Antoniadi One, Mars Base. Standing by for voice contact."

UNSETTLED

LEANA GRIPPED THE BACK OF THE SEAT AS THEY WAITED FOR voices to emerge from the static. Next to her, the boys giggled and bumped each other with their hips.

"Antoniadi One and Two, this is Mars base standing by," Luis said.

Leana scanned the sky for some hint of the incoming craft. Finally, after what seemed an eternity, she noticed a single dark spot.

"Mars base, Antoniadi Two. We read you, Luis. Initiating retro-propulsive descent at five-thousand meters."

"Roger, Antoniadi Two," Luis replied.

"Antoniadi One, Mars base." Leana said. "Standing by for voice contact."

The spot resolved to a ship that fell impossibly far, impossibly fast until finally its engines roared back to life. The ship slowed and stabilized as it descended toward the landing site.

Leana had observed dozens of retro-propulsive landings, but always found the sight incongruous—the way a craft fell out of the sky until, at the very end, it floated to a touchdown on a pillar of fire.

"Antoniadi Two, Mars base standing by." Luis called over the comms.

Finally, Leana spotted the second ship almost past her view through the transport's forward window. *They've overshot the landing!*

"Antoniadi One, Mars base awaiting voice contact." Leana said.

Finally, the ship's engines flared, and it seemed to shudder almost to a stop in midair as it corrected its path and brought itself back to the landing zone.

C'mon, Paul.

"Mars base, this is Antoniadi One," Paul said. "Retro-propulsive descent initiated. How 'bout let's not do that again."

Oh, thank God!

"Antoniadi One, Mars base. It's great to hear your voice, Paul. The hard part's over," Leana said. "Now come on home."

They made it! Leana released her grip on the seat and blood flowed back into her fingertips.

The boys sat, transfixed, as Antoniadi Two was the first to descend on a tower of flame toward the landing area. Dust billowed from beneath the massive ship as her landing struts deployed and she touched down in a cloud.

"Antoniadi Two, Mars base. Touchdown," Luis said. "Welcome to Mars."

The boys high-fived, giggled, and bounced around the cabin.

"That was awesome!" Michael said.

Leana wondered if they understood the significance of all this, and lamented that she might never know. She and Luis had trained for this—had seen the ships land more than a hundred times in the simulator. Michael and Gabriel had just seen it for the first time, and she both adored and envied their naïve excitement. Soon enough, these landings would be just another part of their routine.

Antoniadi One thundered toward the other landing area moments later, and once again the boys were enraptured. It would have seemed like magic to see such an enormous thing hang in the air if not for the incredible noise and wind. Astride chaos, the ship crept downward until her landing struts emerged and she finally touched down.

Luis's uncharacteristic "Whoop!" nearly overloaded her speakers before he killed his transmitter. He shook his hands as if to release the tension.

Leana felt it too. *They're here, and they're safe.* "Alright boys, back in your seats. Let's go get our friends."

Luis packed and loaded the communications gear into his transport's storage compartments. The equipment would soon find other uses, at least until the next group of colonists arrived in about two years.

Luis waved to them again, then climbed the steps into his transport. Leana strapped the boys into their seats, then drove to Antoniadi One's landing area. Soon both vehicles had attached themselves to the ships' extended airlocks.

Leana walked to the airlock door and flashed a smile to her boys. The mixture of excitement and apprehension on their faces stopped her short, and she went to them.

"Boys, there's nothing to worry about." She kneeled and placed her hands on their knees. "Uncle Paul and Aunt Sheila are in there, waiting to see you, and they're going to be so happy to be here."

She, Luis, and Paul had been the driving force behind the entire Mars project, and they'd worked together so closely they were practically family.

"Don't worry, you'll get to know everyone else soon, and there'll be plenty of kids to play with tomorrow once every-one's settled in. Won't that be fun?" They didn't look convinced, but she knew they'd get there. "I love you both. Now, should we let them in?"

Michael tentatively nodded his head.

"OK." Leana patted his leg. "Here we go!"

She approached the door and opened it. On the other side of the airlocks, the ship's occupants were in various states of composure and congratulations. Paul and Sheila stood nearest the door.

Paul's eyes were baggy and red-rimmed, but his huge, familiar grin filled his face as he reached out his hand. "Hey Lee, it's great to see you again."

"Hi, Paul," she said. Instead of offering her hand, she opened her arms and hugged him, then Sheila. "I can't tell you how good it is—and how relieved I am—that you're both finally here." After a moment, she pulled away and said to them and the entire group, "Welcome to Mars. Welcome home."

<hr>

Despite two years of interplanetary separation, Leana marveled at the easy comfort of seeing her friends again.

Paul put his hand on her shoulder and squeezed it congenially. "Everyone," he said as he turned to his crew. "For those of you who've not yet had a chance to meet her, this is Leana Pendrova—my star pupil, my very dear friend, and one of the most capable people I've ever known."

Leana's neck and cheeks flushed. "Welcome to Mars, everyone. We're so happy you're here. Please proceed through the airlock into the transport, and I'll take you to your new homes."

She and her friends had a lot to catch up on, but it could wait.

"Grab your personals, and your helmets," Paul said, "and

let's get out of this bucket!" A wide grin filled his face, and he pulled Sheila into an embrace and a passionate kiss. Some averted their eyes, while others raised their helmets as high as the cramped space allowed and shouted their encouragement.

She led the way into the transport while Paul hung behind to perform his final duties as Antoniadi One's commander.

The crew transports seated forty, so everyone crammed in as best they could. Most found seats, but several chose to stand and hold on to the rails that ran along the ceiling. The boys shared the navigator's seat up front, and Leana introduced them to everyone, though most of them had known both Michael and Gabriel as babies.

His ship empty, Paul boarded the transport and instructed the computer to transfer his ship's final records to the colony's systems for processing and storage, and to prepare it for disassembly.

Both landers were to be dismantled and their parts either re-used elsewhere or broken down into raw materials for the compositors.

The transit structure that had joined the two ships together and served as crew quarters for the past six weeks had been left in orbit. Constructed in space, it was too fragile to survive entry. Still, its materials were precious commodities here on Mars, so it would de-orbit and crash land under computer control and parachutes several kilometers in toward the center of their home crater. Anything that survived entry and impact would mean either more spare parts and fewer things to build from scratch, or more raw materials for the compositors.

Paul took up a position on the rail directly behind the boys, and as he surveyed *Antoniadi One* from the transport's windows, his expression reminded Leana of her own first steps on Mars. She smiled in quiet acknowledgment. *Let him have this moment.* She waited quietly before she took her own seat and turned to address the new colonists.

"Tonight we'll take you to your HABs, where some essential items have been provided. You may request additional supplies through the computer, but if there's something you need urgently, you may retrieve it directly from the storerooms in the Central Pod. Your schedules are in the system, and you should feel free to adjust them through the computer if needed, but I recommend you take this evening to settle in and relax. If you care to join us in the morning, first meal will be at 0600 hours in the Central Pod's cafeteria. After that we'll do a general mission review, individual debriefings, then lunch. Then you'll be on your own to move out and complete your first day's duties. You can direct any questions to your mission commanders, or Luis and I will be available after lunch. Communal meals will be available at 1200 and 1800 hours, though you may elect to take meals in your units if you prefer. As the resident psychologist, I strongly recommend you take every opportunity for social interaction, especially on this first day. The next few months will be busy and personal time at a premium."

These people had trained for this mission for years, so none of this information was new, but there was protocol to follow, and it was usually better to restate things than to assume they were understood.

"We'll get underway now, and we have a quick five-minute drive to the first HAB. Please feel free to ask any questions as we go."

She strapped in and activated the auto-nav program she'd generated to deliver Antoniadi One's crew to their assigned HABs.

As they pulled away, autonomous rovers and disassemblers which had been situated just outside the landing zone came to life. In the rear viewscreen, the rovers retrieved and carried storage capsules away from the ships. Most of these contained personal belongings, equipment, or general supplies, but a select few held seeds, organisms, or genetic material destined for the greenhouse, the eventual green lake, or for The Cradle, their seed vault. They would open all the capsules soon and sort and distribute their contents.

Spidery disassemblers crawled over the ship and removed bolts, panels, and other small components which they would clean and reuse. The ship writhed with activity and blossomed as though in a process of organic decay. Leana switched off the rear viewscreen so the children wouldn't see.

Module by module, Leana welcomed everyone to their new homes and wished them a good night. They'd hit three HABs with surprisingly little jostling for position between stops before Leana realized that Paul had shared her deployment plan with his crew and worked out an efficient first-in, last-out strategy. These new colonists, from many professions, backgrounds, and nations had clearly come together in their years of preparation, and everyone was eager to get settled in. During the short drives between HABs, she, Paul, and Sheila caught each other up on their lives on Earth and Mars—not the stuff that was a matter of record, but the interpersonal things that didn't make it into official reports.

Paul and Sheila's youngest son had gotten married, graduated from college, and embarked on a promising career.

Two families—including a Mission Commander—had been scrubbed from the mission because of an affair, so two other families had been selected to take their place. Leana had known about the personnel changes, but not the reason behind them. Paul did not hide his apparent dislike of the replacement Mission Commander, Charles Durbin, who he blamed for the previous Commander's ouster and whom Leana knew only by reputation.

Jay Stokes, one of the geophysical engineers, had apparently had some kind of religious awakening a year ago, and been unable to contain his enthusiasm, much to Paul's amusement and some of their colleague's annoyance. His zealous evangelism hadn't been enough to get him scrubbed, but it had prompted the mission psychologists to put him through some advanced re-evaluation to confirm his mental fitness.

The last stop was HAB 1, where the Pendrovas had lived since it was completed shortly after their arrival. They occupied Unit A, and Leana had set aside Unit B for the Robinsons.

Paul and Sheila were clearly exhausted, so she showed them around their quarters briefly, then said goodnight and took the boys across their shared central airlock to get ready for bed.

With the boys tucked in and under Nanny's watchful sensors, she drove the transport back to the garage for post-excursion maintenance.

Luis greeted her over the comms as she pulled in.

"It has been quite an evening, hasn't it?" she asked.

"It has indeed." He sounded as tired as she felt. "I'm glad it's done and everyone's made it safe. Now we can begin the real work."

CATASTROPHE

THE NEXT MORNING, LEANA SAT—IN HER FOURTH CONSECUTIVE debrief—so desperately hungry that she only half heard Stephen Miers' story about a contaminated sample container. Despite ten years as a practicing psychologist, this process was far more tedious than she remembered. *Should have taken a break after the last one.*

"…he wasn't even apologetic!" Stephen said, "I was yelling at him when Durbin butted in, shouting at both of us. He dumped all my samples and docked Tony's rations. Tony's a klutz, maybe, but Durbin is just an asshole. He should never have been given command."

Not for the first time today, Leana made a note to follow up with Antoniadi Two's commander, Charles Durbin, once the crew debriefs were concluded.

The door burst open and Tyler Leeds stepped through.

"Ma'am," Tyler said, out of breath. "Dr. Pendrova asked me to come get you. There's a…" He shook his head and seemed to yank back a thought. "something is… you're needed in comms ASAP."

His eyes were wide, his skin ashen, and his voice cracked with what Leana recognized as fear. Her whole body tensed.

"I'm in the middle of a debrief, Tyler. Can you be more specific?"

"I'd rather not, ma'am. It's… it's best you come hear it yourself."

"Well," she said. She tried to keep her own voice measured. "Excuse me, Stephen, we'll have to pick this back up later." She stood and headed for the door, slate in hand. "Alright, Tyler, lead the way." She motioned him through the door, then followed him through the building.

Outside the comms room, Tamra, Tyler's fiancé, sat slumped against the wall, wracked with sobs.

What the hell is going on? Nanny would have notified me if something had happened to the children. She instinctively checked her slate. It showed the boys still in one of the building's meeting rooms with the other children and their new teacher.

Inside, the comms room was choked with tension and despair, punctuated by static and silence. With every second, the static seemed to pull everyone closer to the primary comms panel—everyone but Sheila, who faced away and cried quietly into her hands.

The static cleared with a *-chck-*, and a voice emerged.

…tsunami flooding on coastal areas of eastern Asia and Pacific islands -chck- we have confirmed a high-mass object traveling in excess of three-thousand kilometers per second -chck- The voice was clipped and pitched with tension.

Leana approached Luis and clutched his shoulder. He looked at her, his eyes red, his jaw clenched.

-chck- object now approximately two million kilometers away, will intersect Earth orbital plane in about… five minutes -chck-

Someone in the room sucked in air as if they hadn't in days. Leana struggled to recall the current comms delay. *Six minutes. This message is already six minutes old.* Her knees quivered under a new wave of despair. *Whatever is happening has already happened.*

-chck- multiple major storm systems being tracked planet-wide -chck- tsunami flooding now in... western coastal areas of the United States... low-lying coastal areas completely submerged... -chck-

Sheila gasped and sobbed with a sound like a wounded animal. Tyler and Tamra stood in the doorway, wrapped together.

-chck- distance from earth at intersect will be approximately five million kilometers -chck- oh god... -chck-

Leana's head spun, and at some distant level she realized that she and Luis were wrapped in each other's arms. He clutched at her clothing, as if to close every millimeter of space between them. His arms trembled.

-chck- Lunar colony reports massive tremors -chck- major seismic activity -chck- oh god... oh god... structural and environmental failure -chck-

Leana couldn't breathe. *Devastation.* She couldn't think. *Annihilation.* Her chest constricted, her throat was on fire, and her eyes felt like they might burst. There was another inhuman wail, but this time it was her.

-chck- communications failure with lunar colony -chck- orbital observers report... report... -chck- Their only connection to Earth could not hold back his own tears.

Silence filled the room again for nearly a minute, until a gruff, dispassionate voice broke it. *-chck- Mars colony, this is William Davies of Mission Control. The situation on Earth is dire. -chck- Global storms, tsunami, earthquakes, and volcanic activity have impacted almost the entire world. -chck- Orbital observers have reported the complete destruction of the lunar colony, and in fact, of the moon itself. -chck- Earth's governments have declared a state of global emergency and initiated planetary survival protocols. -chck- In all likelihood, you will be* *on your own for the foreseeable future. -chck- Our hopes and prayers will be with you, as we hope yours will be with us. Good luck. -chck-*

Nothing followed but static.

HELPLESS

The room was unnaturally quiet, as if an explosion had deadened Leana's senses. The life support equipment circulated the air, and people filled the room, but none of the ambient noise registered.

She became aware of Luis' arms around her, and realized that he was all that kept her on her feet. His breath was labored and rapid as he struggled to keep his composure. She embraced him, took her own weight, and leaned back enough to look into his face. Tears welled in his eyes. For a moment, they just looked at each other. She studied the pain written on his face and mapped it onto her heart, and when she turned her face away from his, it was as though she'd torn herself in half.

"Tyler?" Her voice came out almost a whisper.

He struggled to lift his head from Tamra's shoulder and speak. "Yes, ma'am?"

"Are there signals on the official primary or secondary channels?"

He let go of Tamra and wiped tears from his eyes, then

took his seat at the console and checked the displays. "No, ma'am."

"What about backups?" Luis asked. "Are we sure our equipment isn't malfunctioning?"

Tyler touched buttons and screens, and spoke quiet commands. His displays and indicators flickered—red, orange, flashing green, then finally steady green. Numbers, graphs, and wave-forms resumed their motion. "Basic diagnostics indicate zero fault conditions. Equipment appears to be functioning as expected."

"Are the feed repeaters functioning?" Paul asked, standing now with Leana and Luis behind Tyler's chair.

The repeaters were part of an experimental satellite network that provided a continuous connection to Earth's global datanet for non-essential traffic between Earth and Mars. Considered a luxury, it wasn't expected to be widely used or supported back home until the colony had grown.

Tyler pressed more buttons. "They seem to be."

"Let's hear them," Luis said.

All of Earth's live news streams crashed from the speakers at the same time—a mass of chaos and horror. Whatever Leana had expected, it wasn't that.

She and Luis had only activated the system as part of routine tests when just a handful of curated streams were active. Now it seemed to be mostly direct, live feeds from independent reporters. Normally such feeds were managed in real-time by editorial teams, but during major crises some trusted sources were allowed to flow through the system unimpeded. In this case it seemed the floodgates had simply been opened, and since Tyler hadn't thought to isolate a particular feed, everything came through at once.

Everyone cringed from the noise until Tyler reduced the feeds to a more manageable number.

"We have to record this," Leana said.

"Already on it," Tyler replied.

He also separated the feeds aurally, so that each seemed to come from a different part of the room, which made it possible to focus on a single source. Though her ears no longer suffered, the experience was no less painful.

One source described chaos and panic in the streets of New York, while another, having miraculously survived California's quakes and tsunami, described massive destruction and bodies deposited amidst the rubble by receding water.

From mid-continental regions, the reports highlighted confusion, fear, disbelief, and denial. One source claimed to have intercepted a secret government transmission meant for the wealthy and powerful, and was on his way with a group of followers to what he called a "lost hope" facility.

In the room, no one spoke.

Leana's cheeks were wet, but her tears had stopped. She wiped her face while she stood for a moment and watched the others. Their expressions shifted subtly as they changed focus from one source to another, and their brows furrowed and eyes narrowed at each new expression of despair.

These might be Earth's last transmissions, and theirs the only enduring record. The AI could transcribe, catalog, and flag the transmissions which contained the best, most unique information, but eventually, someone would have to review them, and whoever that task fell to would have to endure the tragedy over and over again as they pieced Earth's final hours together for posterity. Tears fell on Leana's cheeks again.

She grasped Luis' arm and turned to face him. She looked into his eyes. "We need to get everyone together." She looked at Paul and Sheila. "We have to tell them what's happened. They deserve the opportunity to hear it for themselves."

FALLOUT

Within fifteen minutes, the entire colony had assembled in the Central Pod's main meeting room. The adults waited impatiently and talked and swapped rumors about what the sudden change of schedule might mean, while the younger children milled about, crawled under chairs, and ran around the back of the room. The older children had gravitated together, annoyed but intrigued enough by the current of tension in the room to wait to see what would happen. Michael and Gabriel had both come to her as soon as they came in with the others, then ran off to be with their new friends.

Now, Leana stood in front of the assembled crowd with Luis, Paul, and Durbin.

They'd discussed how to break the news and agreed that a direct approach was best. Durbin had insisted they stand together to project authority, and Leana agreed under the profession of hope that it might also provide some sense of comfort.

Leana was no stranger to difficult conversations. *But, how do you even begin to soften something like this with platitudes and euphemisms?* She sighed and approached the lectern. *No, direct is the only way.*

"Thank you all for meeting here, on such short notice," she said. "I'm afraid I do not have good news—Earth has suffered a major catastrophe, quite probably an extinction-level event."

The room fell instantly silent, apart from the children's continued play. Shocked expressions filled every face.

"We don't yet know the exact cause, but from the transmissions we've received—and continue to receive—the results are clear. Earthquakes, volcanic activity, and tsunami-like flooding have all contributed to a global tragedy which will very likely render the Earth uninhabitable for at least the next decade."

Gasps and murmurs of confusion swept through the assembly.

"The immediate casualties likely number in the tens of millions. Many coastal areas have been decimated, and earthquakes have leveled inland cities on every continent."

Leana paused for a moment to let them process, but questions and shouts of protest quickly rose from the crowd. She raised her hand in a futile gesture for quiet.

"We do not have a lot of confirmed, specific information. The reports are sporadic and in many cases, inconsistent. Based on what we've heard so far, we believe San Diego and most of LA are flooded, while New York City has come through relatively unscathed. Pacific coastal areas of the Asian continent and islands were among the first to be flooded, but there are reports of survivors in taller buildings that withstood the flooding and the quakes. Atlantic coastal areas seem to have escaped flooding thus far, but rapid sea-level decline has been reported, which suggests that these areas may still be in considerable danger."

She took a breath, only to face an onslaught of raised voices, questions, and fearful speculation.

"Please! Everyone!" She raised her own voice above the crowd and gestured for quiet. After a moment, she continued. "We are still receiving transmissions from Earth, which will be reviewed, cataloged, and preserved. These will, in time, allow us to reconstruct the full scope and timeline of what is happening. This record will be freely available to anyone who needs it. Right now, however, we feel you should be able to hear it for yourselves. This is, perhaps, the gravest tragedy humanity has ever faced, and you… we… need to listen and respond in our own way. Earth may not survive. Humanity's time on Earth may be over. If that is the case—if this is to be the last we hear of our families and friends—we should honor their lives by bearing witness. If we are to be the sole vessel of human history on Earth, we owe it to ourselves to face this tragedy together, with compassion, strength, and respect."

The protests and questions stopped and, apart from those already lost in their sorrow and the children who cried reflexively because of the tension, noise, and fear in the room, the people were quiet.

Perhaps it's why children are so resilient—their emotions are always right at the surface, with no reservations. Leana relaxed her grip on the lectern and breathed.

"Tyler," she said, and the computer routed her voice to the young man's station. "Please let us hear those transmissions in the main meeting room."

FOR OVER AN HOUR, the colonists remained together, huddled around Earth's last transmissions—the desperate sights and sounds of the end of the world.

The comms system's speaker arrays allowed for up to twenty discrete audio transmissions in the large room, which could be attenuated for an individual or a small group. With Leana's help, Tyler localized the transmissions into pools. The Americas and Western Europe took one side of the room, while Eastern Europe, Russia, Africa, and the Middle East took the other. Asia and everything else went to the center. Tyler, with the comms AI's help, tagged every transmission for quality, locale, and language, and only the best, broadly representative transmissions made it into the room as audio. Everything else remained available for private listening.

Many of the colonists floated from one area to another, while others sat transfixed by reports in their native language from their home countries. A few wept over the desperate voices of local celebrities, acquaintances, or friends.

Leana wandered the room to offer help and comfort where she could. She spoke with some and held their hands, touched them, or simply sat with them to reassure them that they were not alone. She brought all her training to bear for them, all while she dangled over the precipice herself.

Nick was in San Francisco, John in Redding. *Underwater, earthquake-prone, surrounded by dormant volcanoes. Gone.* Despair gnawed at her, tore at the edges of her composure. *Be present.* She repeated the phrase like a mantra when she felt the facade slip. *Be present.* She didn't have the luxury to dwell on her father or her brother. *These people need me here, now.* They needed her more now, hopefully, than they ever would again. *Be present.*

Nevertheless, she found herself on multiple occasions transfixed by a familiar voice in the northeast corner of the room. Twenty years ago, the voice had belonged to a young man who was one of the first independent, amateur sources in Redding. Since she'd moved away to college, and then to New Mexico with Luis to bootstrap their Mars dream, his voice had deepened and developed a slow and deliberate weightiness.

But in the face of this tragedy, his carefully cultivated style fell apart. His fear was palpable, his desperation and confusion pitiable, yet he continued to broadcast.

"…making their way to the Sheriff's office. It's still a small group, but more are joining as we walk. The nucleus of this group has apparently learned of a government shelter somewhere in the area, but their contact was cut off before they could learn the location. If there's even a chance…" His voice broke.

His mic and its vocal filters weren't quite enough to remove the voices of those around him, filled with fear and despair.

It would be less cruel if they hadn't heard of the shelter at all, Leana thought. *Perhaps facing a certain reality is better than chasing a false hope.*

"We've been told to go home, that there is nowhere safe to go. If there's even a chance that this shelter exists… we have to try. We've reached the building."

Leana swayed on her feet as if she were suspended from a wire. She probed the empty space between his words. She listened as they entered through unlocked doors. As they strode down empty halls. *C'mon.* As they encountered one empty room after another.

Suddenly her body settled as she realized what it was she was waiting for. *Dad.* Irrationally, she knew, she expected his voice to emerge from the crowd. She expected John Hoffstead to have taken charge, as he always did, to find a way to serve, to lead.

As irrational as it was, she could not move.

"Empty. Even the armory. A couple of people are trying to get into the local datanet, and others are in the records room, but I'm afraid we're out of luck. There's no help here. We're on our own."

Tears streamed down Leana's cheeks, but not for him. Two images filled her thoughts. In one, her mom and dad smiled at her from their side door as she bundled Michael up into the car on the last day of her last visit. Two weeks later she left Earth for Mars. A year later, June's cancer was diagnosed and Leana was stuck on Mars unable to do anything to help. And now. Leana imagined Dad, sad, alone at his kitchen table, scotch in hand, as the world ended around him.

Mel will go to him, surely. Leana considered the possibilities and felt lighter. *Perhaps she'll bring Mary, too.* She imagined the three of them gathered around John's table. Stories. Laughter. Tears. *Together.*

The reporter was out in the streets again. As he walked, he stopped to talk to some he encountered and asked them to share their stories, their sorrows. He seemed determined to leave a record, though Leana wondered who he thought he was leaving it for, how he imagined it would persist. Her heart swelled and tears fell again as she realized it was for her, for them. Perhaps not directly, but... *We are the witnesses.* She understood why they were here. She had said as much before bringing everyone together there. Then it had been a rational proposal, but now she felt it and she wept. *Thank you. Thank you.*

Now this room played host to myriad expressions of human grief. The crying had mostly subsided, but the pain from loss, denial, rage, confusion, and impotence was etched on every face. Most listened quietly alone, or in the company of their partners, while others gathered in small groups of friends or acquaintances. But they were here.

As long as there is room in their hearts to face it together, to not hide from it, but to endure it, there is hope.

It was that human capacity to grasp at hope and optimism that would make Leana's work possible. It was that same capacity within herself that would allow her to stay, emotionally, present enough that she might actually be some help to her fellow survivors.

Nearby, a small group huddled together, deep in some

increasingly agitated discussion, which their body language suggested would soon boil over into a full-fledged argument.

"…and why haven't we heard anything from mission control?" Charles Durbin asked as Leana approached the group. "We should be getting official reports, not listening to this network feed garbage!"

Leana stood for a moment behind Alice and Jay to listen and observe—to take the pulse of the group.

"Yeah, what are they doing down there?" Tony Madia shouted. "They can't leave us alone out here, can they? This is a multi-national mission, surely not everyone has abandoned their posts!"

"No, those bastards have totally forgotten about us," Durbin growled. "The whole organization is a shit-show. Has been from the beginning. We'll be left to fend for ourselves until somebody gets their shit together and remembers that they left us alone up here to die."

"That's a little harsh, maybe, don't you think, Commander?" Alice asked.

"We're never alone…" Jay mumbled.

"No, I don't," Charles interrupted. "They micromanage us within in an inch of our sanity and have contingency plans for every little thing that could go wrong here, but as soon as something unexpected happens there, they shut off the radios and high-tail it. The bastards have cut and run."

"So why are we just sitting around?" Tony asked. "It's like we're witnessing an execution or something! We should be doing something, not sitting on our asses."

"What would you have us do, Tony?" Leana asked.

Charles glared at her.

So… not a fan. It's okay, I don't much care for you either.

"Get some damned answers, for a start." Tony said, but his aggressive bravado collapsed when he realized who had asked the question. "Find out if we're really on our own here, I guess, or if we can expect a resupply mission once whatever this is has blown over."

"The communications team is already working to re-establish contact," Leana said. "They're also trying to tap into Earth-local satellite and data feeds to find out what we can. Unfortunately, only a handful of us are qualified to do that work. So, if this is really the end of humanity on Earth, rather than ignoring it, we should be present for it—we should listen and honor…"

"Bullshit!" Charles interrupted. "If Earth is dead or dying, we should do everything we can to make sure **we** aren't. We need to move up our timetables or risk running out of damned food and oxygen. We should be out there doing our damned jobs, not sitting here crying over something we can't do anything about."

"Charles, no one is forcing you to be here," Leana said. "Stay or go, it's up to you. However, please understand that some of us need time to deal with this grief and would not do as well if they, as you said, 'cut and run' from this tragedy."

"Bah," Charles huffed.

"The Holy Mother will protect us," Jay said. "All we…"

"They haven't 'cut and run,'" Alice interrupted. "If they activated the Arks, they would have evacuated critical personnel to them. There's just no one left on the outside to get our messages."

Everyone stared at Alice like she'd spit out centipedes.

"Oh, uh, I was on the team responsible for planning and design of the Carolina Ark after college," she said. "In a national emergency, key military and governmental personnel and their families, including CNSEA personnel—would be sent there."

"You **knew** about these things?" Charles shouted, and his finger trembled, a foot from Alice's face. "Why didn't you say anything before now?"

"What good would it have done?" Alice's face flushed, but she didn't flinch.

"Maybe we could have gotten messages to our… people, told them where to go! Did you think about that?" Durbin's hesitation caught Leana's attention. Unless she mis-remembered, he had no family to speak of.

"Of course I did! But Leana made it clear that we're cut off!" Alice seemed about to explode. "Don't you think I've thought about what I could do if I weren't here? It's all I **can** think about! My whole family is down there. I could be taking them to safety, but **I'm not there**! I'm stuck up here, helpless, just like you!"

Leana put her hand on Alice's shoulder. "Please, everyone," she said, "this isn't productive."

"Damn right," Charles grumbled.

"Charles! That is enough," Leana said. "If there's something you'd rather be doing, go do it! There's certainly enough work to go around. As a Mission Commander, you have the authority to put together a work detail and get started on whatever you feel is more worthwhile. If you want to stay here, that's fine too, just shut the hell up, because all you **are** doing is upsetting people."

Leana's fingers trembled and her heart raced. *Probably could have handled that better.* She tried to find the source of the anger that had leaped out of her just then, but there was nothing. *Must be his smug face and grating personality.*

"As if you care," Charles said as he stood. "You brought your family with you. You didn't sacrifice anything to be here. Screw you." He stormed away and left the room entirely.

Leana thought again of John, Nick, and Mel. Of Luis' family. *You have no idea, asshole.* She thought of Michael and Gabriel who weren't quite old enough to understand the full meaning of what had happened.

Around the room, all the grief-stricken faces shared a sense of being in free-fall. The same precipice lay before her, and she could so easily give herself over to it. *You have no idea.*

Tony broke the silence. "So..." he began, "if they've evacuated critical personnel, mission control is effectively shut down, right? We really are alone up here, aren't we?"

Alice confirmed the question with a nod, her scowl undiminished, and Tony sunk even further into his chair.

$$\overline{}$$

ALONE

$$\overline{}$$

LUIS PACED THE ROOM, HIS BROW FURROWED AND HIS FACE fixed with a scowl. "Well, where is it?"

"I'm still scanning the area," Tyler said as his fingers flew over the console and rows of numbers scrolled across his screens.

The target of their search—LaLDOP 5—was the nearest of two orbital platforms positioned in the Earth/Sun Lagrange points L4 and L5. The twin platforms hosted, among many other systems, the Gemini Deep Space Telescopes, which together formed one of the most powerful observatories in the history of astronomy.

"It can't have gone far, can it?" The tension in Tyler's voice ground against Luis' own.

"Who knows!" Luis stopped behind Tyler's chair and sighed. "What we do know is that a super-massive object passed through the solar system. An object that massive— massive enough to destroy the moon—could have yanked the platform out of L5, possibly out of the system altogether." Luis leaned in and rested his hands on the back of Tyler's seat.

"Regardless, it **is** out there somewhere, and if we can find it, maybe it can help us figure out what's going on."

Luis forced himself to relax and step away. He resumed pacing.

Tamra turned her chair in Luis' direction as he passed behind her. "I've run a simulation of orbital dynamics during the event. It may help." She didn't sound convinced.

Luis stepped up behind her as she turned back to her screens, and he watched the representation of planets and other objects move in their orbits.

"See here, when whatever it was passed through, the moon would have been almost opposite the Earth from L5." Tamra's finger trembled as she pointed out the objects on her screen. "We don't know enough about the object or it's trajectory, but it would have to have passed close by the moon to have caused its destruction. It may have had little effect on the platform—if anything, it may have pulled the platform closer to Earth as it passed, or down, out of the orbital plane as it approached."

Tyler made adjustments to his console. "I've hijacked a few of CNSEA's Earth orbital satellites and am sending them instructions to help locate the platform," he told Luis without taking his eyes off his screens. "I patched command and control through the quantum radio. It's low bandwidth, so we won't be able to retrieve data that way, but I can at least send instructions and get basic status readouts in near-real-time."

"Excellent. Good thinking," Luis said.

The experimental quantum radio was not yet fully field-tested and certified for use. No doubt Tyler had already bypassed the system's restrictions, so Luis kept quiet and let the man do his job.

"Tamra, while he's hunting L5, why don't you see what else those satellites can tell us over the standard channels."

Within moments, a distinctive ping prompted Tyler into a flurry of activity.

"I think…" Tyler tapped out more commands, "yes! We've found it!"

"What's its story, Tyler?"

"Let's see…" he said, "the course-correction system **is** active. There's a positional alert, which likely means it's having trouble holding orbit inside L5. We won't know more until we get full telemetry over standard. It's reporting an error on the link with L4."

"Well, we'll worry about that later," Luis responded. "We have one great big eye, let's see what it can do."

Tyler commanded the observatory to point toward Earth, away from the depths of space. "Positive response to commands, but we won't get data for another… seven to eight minutes."

Seven to eight minutes to stew on too many questions, for which Luis had too few answers. Still, questions helped the scientist in him—the rationalist—hold at bay the parts of him that wanted to submerge into the despair that lapped at his heart.

"Come on!" Tamra muttered, "Where are you?"

Luis breathed. "What've you got?" He leaned in to get a closer look at her displays.

Tamra shrugged and waved her hands at them. "Nothing… just, nothing. I've got everything looking where the moon should be, and there's just nothing there! Nothing visible, nothing in infrared, UV, or even X-ray! No debris, no residual heat. It's not like it disappeared… it's like it was never there to begin with!"

She growled and tears streamed across her cheeks as she jammed at the buttons. She'd had family at one of the lunar colonies.

Luis tried to keep the tension out of his voice—she'd be little good to him if she couldn't calm down and stay focused.

He put his hand atop her shoulder to offer comfort. "How far from its expected position have you looked?"

"Most of these observations cover a ten to twenty-degree field of view," she replied and wiped tears from her face. "But I've pushed some of them to nearly sixty. If there's anything within a few hundred thousand kilometers, we should see it."

"From all the reports, I don't think we should expect to find much. The moon and her colonies are gone. We will take time to mourn them later. For now, let's get all eyes on Earth."

She looked up at him and he at her, and he tried to convey sympathy, presence, comfort, and strength in a glance. *We will mourn them later.* She seemed to understand, and turned back to her console.

Luis thought about his and Leana's home in New Mexico. Thought about their family, their neighbors, their little town. Too many questions. Not enough answers. *How can we help if we don't even know what's going on?*

Long ago, Leana had helped him recognize that problem solving was his number one coping mechanism. *Just as well. Now is the time for coping.*

He realized Tamra was speaking and he wasn't listening. He wrestled his focus back to the room.

"... weather, news, and private mapping satellites sending me data. I have a few pictures already, but honestly, there's so much cloud cover I haven't been able to identify **any** surface features."

"Let's see what you've got." They'd all surfed waves of adrenaline and despair for nine hours straight. Fatigue pulled at him.

Tamra stepped through satellite imagery on her monitors. Luis' confusion grew until he remembered, "There were reports of widespread volcanic activity. This isn't normal cloud cover. Do we have anything that'll show us infrared?"

She pulled up another set of images that showed an orange

field peppered with areas that transitioned from orange to red, yellow, and white.

"What are we looking at?"

Tamra brought up an overlay of text and the outlines of continents and political boundaries on the image. Near the bottom, off-centered, an elongated white spot was labeled "Hawaii." Yellow and red trailed from the white off the edge of the image.

"Holy crap," Tamra muttered.

Must have gone up like a roman candle.

Several more white spots dotted the North American northwest, the largest of which dwarfed all the others. *Yellowstone.* Near the western Pacific coast snaked a bright orange-to-red line that had to be the San Andreas.

"Every potential volcano on the planet must have erupted." Luis' voice wavered as he struggled to process what he saw. "The atmosphere must be choked with soot and ash. That's why they opened the Arks—the surface will be uninhabitable for decades, at least."

"That's not the half of it," Tyler said. His console flickered with a flow of data as he worked the controls. "Data's started to come in from Gemini."

A shiver ran up Luis' spine. "And?"

"Preliminary readings indicate…" Tyler checked his screens again. "Earth's orbit has increased by," his voice faltered, "shit—almost a million kilometers, and its inclination is approaching ten degrees." Tyler dropped his hands to his lap as he sat back in his chair, his shoulders slumped. Tamra's hand covered her mouth as tears streamed down her face.

The dull ache that had settled into Luis' chest now gripped and twisted him into a knot of despair.

Farther from the sun and with global cloud cover, Earth's temperature would drop dramatically and the surface would freeze in a matter of months, maybe weeks. A new Ice Age was inevitable. Recovery, impossible. Whatever hope Earth had was gone.

"Luis, I don't know how much more we can handle," Leana said.

Her eyes were red and her voice was strained. She'd been with the other colonists all day, helping as much as she could, but Luis knew what a strain that had to have been on her. He was glad she was here.

They sat in front of his desk in his office, her hands in his. He reached up to wipe an errant tear from her cheek.

"I know, sweetie, but we owe it to them to try to learn all we can."

He had sent her, Paul, and Durbin all the information he and his team had uncovered so far, and their conclusions about the bleak outlook for Earth.

"I can't even **process** it!" She yanked her hands away and slashed at the air emphatically. "My family! My brothers, Mel, Dad? Your family!? It's too much!" She sat back in her chair, deflated.

"I know. I'm…" his voice caught in his throat. "I've been trying not to think about it."

"Hold me?" she took his hands again and stood.

Luis stood, stepped into her arms, and held her as closely as he could. She nuzzled into his neck and he felt the wetness of her cheek between them, and the warmth of her breath on his collar. This was one of the very few places he felt he could stay forever.

He relaxed into her and a wave of vertigo hit him. Thoughts passed through his mind—his mom's joy at meeting Leana, her seeing how happy Leana made him, and her unspoken approval every time she caught the two of them sharing an affectionate moment. His throat closed around the certainty that his mom would be glad they were alive, here, together. He hugged Leana even tighter and clutched at her clothing, holding on to her with everything he was. She squeezed him back, and the knot of despair that crushed his chest released ever so slightly.

The door opened and someone started to come in, stopped, fumbled over an apology, and backed out. Luis' eyes were closed and his head turned from the door, but they expected Paul, and his voice was unmistakable. Luis gave his wife another quick squeeze, then began to release and separate from her. He met her eyes, reached up to caress and dry her cheeks, and kissed her lips, cheek, and forehead. He held her gaze for a moment and attempted to transmit the love, gratitude, empathy, compassion, and understanding he felt through the air to her.

Never satisfied, he nevertheless turned his eyes toward the door. "It's okay, Paul, you can come on in."

Paul entered with a sheepish look of understanding and apology that carried through his whole body. "Sorry," he said, "didn't mean to intrude."

"No, no, it's okay," Leana said. "We were expecting you."

"You looked over the data I sent?" Luis asked and gestured to one of the chairs in front of his desk.

"Yeah," Paul said as he sat. "It's terrifying! How sure are we of this? Is there a chance you're wrong?"

"There are a lot of uncertainties still," Luis said. "We've made the most of the data we could get, which runs the gamut but isn't super deep. We need to continue observations and get more data before we'll know for sure."

"Just before I came here, Tyler noticed that the comms lag time wasn't what it should be… he's tracking that too, to see if it can shed some light."

"But the bottom line is, Earth appears to be headed for

another Ice Age," Paul said. "I'm not sure what we can do for them, even if we were to reestablish contact." He paused and leaned back in his chair. "If there's anyone left to reestablish contact with."

"I have to believe that there is." Luis walked around his desk and sat in his chair. "We know some made it underground. Even if all we do is help them understand what's happened, what's happening, we owe it to them."

"But right now the bigger question is, what happens to us?" Leana said, and raised her hands as if to shrug. "We are on our own here, and we're not ready."

Luis held up a hand. "Durbin's not here yet, should we wait for him?" Luis asked.

"Screw that guy," Paul said, his eyes fixed on a spot on the floor.

Luis' raised his eyebrows, "Not a fan?"

"Not even a little." Paul stiffened as he spoke. "Not after what he put us through the last couple of months before launch."

"You mentioned something about that on arrival day," Leana exhaled heavily. "We'd read about the personnel changes, of course, but we didn't hear any of the backstory."

"I'll fill you in later," Paul said, "over a stiff drink." He held up both hands. "I don't have the stomach for it right now. Suffice it to say, Durbin is a capital-D Dick."

Again, Luis' eyebrows shot up. *Durbin must have really pissed him off, he's not usually so prickly.*

"Okay…" Leana echoed Paul's gesture. "Okay." She also seemed to have been caught a little off-guard. "We have six months of supplies, maybe a year if we engage in some strict rationing, and we can't expect any help from Earth."

"Certainly not within the next six months," Luis said. "And unless our data is severely flawed, probably not… ever, in all likelihood."

"So we're a hundred percent on our own," Leana said, "and according to current schedules, we're at least six months out from completing the greenhouse expansions and establishing the green lake. A year—at best—from complete self-sufficiency." She leaned forward in her chair, forearms on her legs, her palms together. She stared ahead with the unfocussed look of contemplation.

"We've got quite a few things ready to harvest in the existing greenhouse," Luis looked toward Paul, but in truth, his attention was still on Leana in his periphery. "but that was never intended to sustain more than our family for any length of time."

"My people are ready for all contingencies, including rationing," Paul stated. "They knew the risks."

"But if we can avoid it, or at least curtail it, we should." Leana's voice was distant.

Luis and Paul both held silent for a moment and shifted their attention to Leana. They both knew her well enough to understand that her tone was preparatory.

"If we're to survive this," she straightened and placed her hands on her thighs, "we've got to have food and we've got to have oxygen—we've got to have the green lake, **now.**" She held Luis' gaze in that way she had when she wanted to make sure he heard and understood her. "We've got to put everything into it—rearrange work schedules, redirect all but the most essential resources, get every compositor we have pumping out parts. The lake will give us raw materials for our food compositors and it will generate oxygen, but we need it operational within the month if we have any hope of reaching sustainability before our supplies run out."

"Within the month!" Paul sat up, his eyes wide. "Even our most pessimistic contingencies didn't suggest attempting to build the dome in a month!"

"The contingencies didn't cover the current situation—I

know," Luis said, "I wrote most of them, and every one included at least one unmanned supply drop within a year."

"I'm not suggesting this lightly," Leana said. "In the short term, we'll have to sacrifice tremendously to make this work. We'll expend more of our resources more quickly, but it will gain us security for the future."

"And if it fails?" Paul asked.

"Well, it will hardly matter, will it?" Leana looked at her hands. "We either run hot and risk shortening our time here, or we give up and let the inevitable come." She fixed her eyes on Paul. "I know I would rather take the risk and try, than to sit back and do nothing."

Paul watched her for a moment then looked at Luis.

"You know she's right, Paul." Luis nodded his head ever so slightly in Leana's direction. "It's the only way."

"Yes, of course she's right." Paul leaned back in his chair again and sighed. "She's always right."

Leana grabbed her slate off Luis' desk and pulled her stylus from her pocket. She gestured to connect her slate to Luis' and Paul's, and scribbled wildly. "First," she said, "we focus on the dome..."

GROUNDED

Like many of the colonists, Leana had kept the vigil for Earth all night, while others left to escape their frustration or to begin their work. She spoke individually to many who stayed to help them process their grief until she'd begun to feel worn smooth by the constant emotional flow.

The room was quiet this morning except for the last few transmissions that trickled in. Most of those who stayed had moved from fear and despair to unity, strength, and conviction. She was heartened to witness their emotional fortitude and ability to accept grief with a measure of self-awareness. Grief lingered in all their faces, which they would carry for a long time to come. She only hoped they were all strong enough for the work that lay ahead.

With Luis and Paul flanking her, she approached the rooms' lectern, and Tamra patched her into comms so everyone in the colony could hear.

"Everyone, this is Leana Pendrova." She paused for a moment as those in the room turned to give her their attention. "By now you've heard the findings from our communications team, and understand more about the dire situation facing Earth. We will continue our observations to get a clearer picture of her fate as the days progress," Leana said. "We'd also like to ask for volunteers… for people to research ways to aid Earth's recovery, or at least to help cope with what's happened. Our colony exists to breathe life into a dead world, perhaps we can use that expertise to save a living one.

"In the meantime," she continued, "our own situation is no less dire. With no resupply from Earth, we are on our own. And, even with extensive rationing, our supplies will very likely not hold out long enough to meet our self-sufficiency milestones. But all is not lost. Paul and Luis and I," she gestured to her husband and her friend beside her, "met last night to discuss these realities, and we agreed on a plan to accelerate our timetables for certain critical projects."

Leana stepped out from behind the lectern. "We need to radically increase our capacity to replenish our oxygen and provide food, and the green lake is our best bet and our highest priority. The lake and its algae will produce oxygen and can also serve as raw material for our food compositors. We intend to have the lake filled, and the dome completed and ready to pressurize and seed within the month."

There were more than a few shocked faces in the crowd. At the back of the room, Charles Durbin entered with a scowl.

"This will not be easy. We all will be asked to make sacrifices over the next several months." Leana clasped her hands. "We're asking for volunteers to join the dome-building effort. The original team of engineers assigned to the green lake and dome construction will be divided into three shifts, and we'll need volunteers to fill out each of those shifts—the more, the better. Volunteers will still be expected to perform your existing duties in a reduced capacity."

Leana glanced at Luis, who stepped toward her as she

continued. "Everyone will be asked to work more hours, which may be difficult for some, but we hope everyone will step up to ease the general workload in order to best support our volunteers in their expanded duties."

Apart from a small group that had gathered around Jay Stokes in the back of the room and whispered amongst themselves, the crowd seemed attentive and determined. *So far, so good.*

"A few of our volunteers may be assigned to the geo and environmental science teams according to their backgrounds and interests, to help find ways we might help Earth's survivors. The rest will support dome construction, and prepping and filling the lake. Your preferences will be taken into consideration, of course, but the colony's self-sufficiency is our priority." Leana stepped aside. "Unless there are any questions, you can register your volunteer status with your AI while Luis reviews the initial team breakdowns."

Charles Durbin stepped up behind the last row of chairs and spoke up. "So, there's not even going to be any discussion about this? You're just going to arbitrarily and unilaterally modify our daily work schedules?"

"Your fellow Mission Commanders agreed this was the best approach to get us up and running as quickly as possible," Leana said.

"Mission Commanders! The 'mission' is over! The Earth is gone, and the CNSEA with her. There **is** no mission!"

"You are welcome to put together a team of your own, Mission Commander." *Maybe a little too much salt on that one...* "I'm sure the colony will accommodate any reasonable pursuits that do not hinder the primary goal of self-sustainability."

"That is not the point, and you know it," Charles said. "This should have been a community decision from the beginning."

"Thanks for your input, Charles," Leana said. "Now, if you don't mind, let's proceed, and we can discuss plan adjustments after everyone has their assignments." She gestured to Luis, who stepped up to the lectern as Charles grumbled and folded his arms.

"Thanks," Luis said as he tapped a few buttons on the lectern to pull up his notes. "As Leana said, we'll be breaking the greenhouse team into three shifts, shooting for full specialty coverage each shift. Work assignments will shift as the project progresses, so at some point you **will** be asked to complete tasks outside of your specific training and areas of specialization. To avoid burnout, you'll rotate duties every few days, but if you'd prefer to stay on a particular task longer, just say the word. Those of you who choose to volunteer will continue your normal duties on a reduced four-hour schedule, arranged around your volunteer schedule."

Leana watched the room as Luis spoke and, despite her best efforts, her eyes repeatedly returned to Durbin, whose face grew redder by the moment until finally he turned and left the room in a huff.

Luis paused and scanned the rest of his notes. "Everyone will get some downtime, at least six hours of sack time, and scheduled mealtimes. If you need special considerations, let us know and we'll work it out. Any questions?"

No hands raised.

"All right then," he said. "Team assignments."

Luis called out each member of the greenhouse team and their new shift assignments.

LEANA AND LUIS walked toward their offices down a corridor that normally felt claustrophobic, yet now it seemed perilously expansive. Luis felt miles away, and she reached across the chasm of space to take his hand. His warmth was a balm to whatever part of her had contracted in the almost twenty-four hours since…

"Your hands are warm." She interrupted herself, and in the seconds that followed, half expected her voice to echo back to her in the cavernous hall.

He looked at her and smiled. Everything about him comforted her—not just the way he looked at her, but the way he walked next to her; the way he held the space between them not as a barrier, but as a closed circuit, full of energy.

Leana relaxed back into the world—back into herself—and the world held him closer to her.

As they approached the split in the corridor that would take them to their separate offices, the comms chimed.

"Go ahead," Luis said.

"Luis…" the comms system manifested Paul's voice as though he were standing directly in front of them. "You'd better get down here. My office."

Leana had known Paul long enough to recognize the exasperation in his voice. She and Luis shared a glance. *He heard it too.*

"We're on our way."

"Leana's with you. Good. Saves me a call."

They turned down the hallway toward Paul's office. Raised, agitated voices careered down the corridor from Paul's open door. Luis, at Leana's side, audibly groaned. He sucked in a breath as they stepped into the room.

"Goddamnit, Paul! We knew the risks and the sacrifices we would be asked to take on for the colony's benefit, but it's another thing altogether to ask us to sacrifice for a lost cause!"

"We don't know if Earth is a lost cause yet," Leana said, as she stepped into the center of the room, not quite between Durbin and the desk Paul was seated behind.

Durbin didn't waste the opportunity to focus on a new

target. "Oh, c'mon! We've all seen the same reports. Earth is dead, and it's only a matter of time before anyone still clinging to life there will be too."

Leana realized—too late—that she should, perhaps, have taken a less aggressive approach. It surprised her—the force of will required to **not** slap the shit out of him. Luis jumped in before she could give in to the urge.

"Yes, Charles, we **have** seen the same reports," Luis said, "but we also have some of the brightest scientific minds *here*, alive and well, and we may still be able to find a way to help Earth's survivors."

"Earth was still recovering from the last global climate disaster we narrowly averted," Durbin scoffed, "and we don't have resources here to spare."

"Here, no," Paul agreed. "But we can spare the brainpower to figure out if the Earth still has resources **they** could tap into."

"Bah!" Durbin exclaimed. "*If* you can actually come up with something that might work, and *if* they can gain access and control of the resources! By the time all the pieces are in place, it will be too late, and all you'll have done is squander time and effort that could have been spent **here** ensuring *our* survival!"

"Commander Durbin is right," Tony Madia spoke up from outside their little circle, "but I think we're missing the point here, aren't we?"

"Yes, right, of course." Charles shot Tony a dangerous look. "You claim this is a decision of the Mission Commanders, and yet you saw fit to exclude me from the discussion."

"You were invited, Charles, but you didn't show up or even acknowledge our message," Leana said. "We waited as long as we felt was reasonable."

"Besides," Paul said, "you took the position in the final stages of the project under dubious circumstances, at best."

Leana fixed Paul with a look. *And apparently he's just going to ignore me.*

"Crises seem to have a way of manufacturing themselves around you…" Paul finished.

"Ha! Well…" Charles fumbled around a response. "You… you know this is meant to be a civilian colony, anyway. The point, *Doctor* Pendrova, *Doctor* Robinson," his voice dripped with sarcasm, "the *point* is that you're still trying to run this colony like a CNSEA mission." Charles tapped two fingers forcefully on top of Paul's desk. "The colony charter specifies that a civic council is to be established upon our arrival. We have the right to self-govern—to not be treated like slaves."

"Now, wait just a damned minute!" Paul jumped to his feet, red-faced, and nearly toppled his chair.

Leana held out a hand to dissuade him. "No, Paul, he's right."

As much as Durbin made her want to punch something, continued escalation would not help the situation.

And Durbin wasn't wrong about the civic council. Things **had** felt off since the tragedy—the Mission Commanders had never been intended to play the role of colony administrators. They had stepped up to lead through this crisis, like they had trained to do, but, ultimately this was not their crisis to manage —it was the colony's.

"He's… what?" Paul stammered.

She shared another look with Luis, full of meaning.

"He's right," Luis repeated. "We've overstepped our authority."

Paul collected himself and shook his head. "No. **Bullshit.**" He looked at Leana. "Our *job* is to make the schedules and keep the colony functioning until the civic authority is established."

Charles stood quietly with crossed arms and a slight smirk.

"Yes," Leana replied, "and it's our **responsibility** to

ensure that happens in a timely fashion, before any far-reaching decisions are made."

"Well, yes, but…"

"Charles is correct." Luis said.

Durbin outright grinned.

"Computer," Luis said, "voice transmission to all colonists."

A fraction of a second later, the AI's standard voice stated, "Open."

"Everyone, this is Luis Pendrova. In accordance with our colony charter, nominations for Civic Council are now open. The computer will accept nominations until Sol 734. Voting will open on Sol 734 starting at 0800 hours and conclude at 2100 or once all the colony's votes have been cast. The positions of Council Chairperson and Council Representatives will be determined through preferential voting, so please rank all candidates for Council in order of your choice for Chairperson."

Charles' grin faded.

"Satisfied?" Luis asked.

Durbin nodded, turned, and left the room. His companions trailed behind.

"Charles will nominate himself," Paul retook his seat. "He's been jockeying for authority since he joined the project. You have to have seen that." He leaned back in his chair.

"We could do worse than Charles Durbin," Leana said. She almost snorted at the shock on Paul's face as he sat up straight again. She held up her hands for patience. "Yes, he's a blowhard, and a self-important ass, but at least **here** he's operating in the colony's best interests."

"You haven't worked with him for the past two years. He may be a more or less competent engineer, but he's unstable and I don't trust him. He *thinks* he is protecting the colony's interests," Paul tapped his temple, "but in any kind of leadership position, he would push too hard and risk destroying everything we're trying to achieve."

"Which is precisely why we need a council—to keep people like Charles Durbin in check." Leana replied. *Hopefully, at any rate…*

CHANGES

The chaos of lunchtime conversation drifted through Luis' door as it opened to admit Svetlana Popovna and Tyler Leeds. Lana carried a slate and a perplexed expression, while Tyler looked as exhausted as Luis felt.

The simple facts of life on Mars—the pressure suits, recycled air, claustrophobia-inducing humidity, and the ever-present martian regolith—were enough to wear a person down, even with their previously ambitious shifts of only 6 hours. Now that a solid majority of them had taken on at least a partial extra shift and fewer hours of downtime per day, they were all exhausted.

"What can I do for you two?"

There was something between the way Lana looked at him; her subversive, arid humor; and her unassuming earnestness, that often made it difficult for Luis to take her seriously. In the week since she'd arrived, he'd found that she left him perpetually in want of a punchline.

"We have... uh..." she appeared to search for a word, "mystery."

After ten years as a student and scientist in Europe and

America, Lana's Russian accent had softened, but she'd not lost it altogether. Despite her fluency with English—and the five other languages she also spoke—she still would occasionally misuse words or drop them altogether, which lent her speech an unpredictable, musical quality that Luis enjoyed.

"A mystery, eh?" Luis asked. "You mean something more mysterious than usual?"

Despite eighty-plus years of orbiters, landers, and rovers, Mars was still largely unexplored. Unraveling her mysteries was a big part of why they were here. At least, it **had been**.

For the moment, Martian mysteries may have to take a back seat.

"Yes, precisely," she replied.

Luis tried to keep the smirk off his face—his loose attempt at humor hadn't landed. Her brow was still creased, and she held the slate and glanced at it as if to confirm it still said what she thought it said.

"My findings are still… preliminary," she said, "but I have double-checked them, and compared against available records."

Luis set his slate atop a tray of soil samples and rested his clasped hands on top of what was now the one clear spot on his desk, which was covered with the detritus of two isolated years of research, experimentation, and simple tinkering. He looked up at her with what he hoped was an expression of patience.

"It is getting warmer," she said, "the whole planet. All readings indicate it is a one-half degree-warmer than it should be. I cannot explain this, but I have been unable to conclude… differently."

Next to her, Tyler looked up from his slate and his apparent fatigue gave way to attentive listening.

From someone without her credentials, Luis would have assumed this to be frivolous conjecture; but her reputation as a climatologist was why he'd persuaded her to join his mission to establish the first permanent Martian colony. If she wasn't certain of her findings, and concerned by them, she would have filed them with her normal reports, not walked them into his office.

Still, his confidence in her did not prevent him from asking, "Are you certain?"

"Very. I double-check everything, and ask Roger to double-check also."

"I have no doubt," Luis said. "So, what do we **know**?"

"Only that global temperatures and atmospheric pressures have risen continually since the event. We have not determined yet any other direct cause." She frowned and pushed her screen of data to his slate. "It appears to be a consistent, gradual change, rather than the result of some intermittent activity. Geology team has ruled out large-impact or volcanic events. Essentially, we know nothing useful. Yet."

"OK, well, if you can't determine a cause, what can you tell me about the effect?"

Tyler's attention had given way almost to agitation.

"As I said, it has been a consistent but gradual change, such that our weather analysis software didn't pick it up." She pushed more data to his display. "I only discovered it when I saw anomaly in annual comparison data—the last five years have been consistent, after accounting for measurable external factors, but the last six days have not fit pattern. When I looked closer, I saw increasing disparity…"

Luis flipped through the data. Such a small change was hardly something to worry about, but the trend was clear.

"Uh, if I may, sir… Lana…" Tyler flicked data from his slate to theirs. "You know we've been doing orbital analysis, among other things, since the event. It's why I'm here, sir. I finally have enough data to extrapolate some things…"

"Well, spit it out, Tyler."

"Well," Tyler replied, "if my numbers are correct, the

Earth is about twelve degrees above the ecliptic, and her orbital position is almost nineteen million kilometers beyond aphelion. As near as I can tell, that equates to a solar-relative velocity between forty and forty-three kilometers per second."

"Shit," Luis muttered.

Lana's expression suggested puzzlement. Luis gestured for Tyler to explain.

"At this point, the Earth **may have** enough velocity to escape the solar system altogether."

Lana's eyes widened in understanding.

"But it sounds like you're not sure," Luis said.

"Well, see, here's the other thing," Tyler replied. "It's been hard to get a precise reading because... well... the stars aren't exactly where they're supposed to be."

Luis' head spun, but he stayed quiet.

"Typically, we understand our position and the position of other objects through various means including radio triangulation, and, for visible objects, by triangulating against known intra and extrasolar objects." Tyler continued, "Except, now, almost nothing is where it's supposed to be, especially local objects. Deep-field reference objects are off too, but not by as much. None of the observations line up properly." Tyler's tone suggested a theory—his voice was bright despite these dire pronouncements. He swallowed and coughed—he practically vibrated. "As near as I can tell—and we'll need more observations to confirm it—but it seems that Mars' orbit has shifted as well."

In light of the massive change in the Earth's orbit, this news was hardly unexpected, which didn't explain Tyler's barely restrained excitement.

"And you seem to think this is good in some way?"

"Possibly, yes," Tyler replied. "Possibly very good. Before this event, Mars orbited at the far edge of the habitable zone, but based on these numbers our orbit has shrunk, possibly to as close as one hundred ninety million kilometers, while orbital velocity has increased. We're looking at five hundred sol years, give or take."

Now it was Lana's turn to perk up. Her eyes brightened with understanding.

"Of course, it all depends on the orbital eccentricity," Tyler continued, "which has almost certainly changed. We won't know for sure until we get more data."

"So Earth **may** be getting ejected from the solar system, while Mars has been pulled closer to the sun?" Luis asked.

"This likely explains temperature shifts!" Lana said.

"That's what I was thinking," Tyler replied.

"So, if orbit stabilizes, temperatures stabilize, we have warmer Mars." Lana's face scrunched for a second as she thought. "This also explains atmospheric pressure changes as well. More sunlight means more sublimation of polar caps, and warmer Mars means more melting of subsurface ice."

"If the orbit stabilizes," Luis said.

"There's a chance, if my numbers are NOT correct," Tyler said, "that Mars' orbital changes continue until we end up in a close solar orbit inside the habitable zone, or get too close and fall into the sun or get spun farther out like the Earth."

"Too close," Svetlana picked up the thread, "temperatures continue to rise and Mars' weak magnetosphere allows atmosphere boil off faster from increased solar wind."

"Well," Luis said, "I'm just not sure how I feel about all this. Keep your eyes on it and keep it to yourselves until we get more data. Our people have enough on their minds."

"Understood," Lana said, and Tyler nodded. They turned and left Luis without so much as a smirk.

Luis knocked a sharp pattern on Paul's open door frame and poked his head around a moment later. A dark scowl occupied Paul's face.

"Hey Paul, got a second?"

Paul's attention remained fixed on the slate in his hands. He grunted gruffly and gestured for Luis to enter.

Luis walked in and took a seat in front of Paul's desk. Paul continued to scroll through information on his slate as though he wasn't even aware Luis was there.

The desk was virtually empty—even after a week of occupation—though a box of ephemera sat on a chair by the far wall and an unlabeled manilla envelope lay on the desk, still tied closed. The envelope had a pack and track sticker from the colonists' load-out, and the words "Office" and "Photos" written on it in black marker. Paul's office was a stark contrast to Luis' own, but then he'd had two years to break his in.

Luis cleared his throat quietly. "Uh, I can come back later, if you're busy."

"What? No. It's fine." Paul placed the slate on his desk but didn't deactivate it or even pretend to move it out of view. "Please," he said as he adopted a more attentive posture, "what can I do for you?"

"Well, I have some updates you'll want to hear, that I want to pick your brain over."

"Okay, shoot."

As Luis relayed the news and conclusions Svetlana and Tyler had presented, Paul's eyes flicked to the slate's display which continued to update every few seconds. Paul grunted and vocalized at points to indicate attentiveness, but it was clear that his attention was still divided.

"So," Luis said, after a brief pause, "may I ask what it is that has you so distracted?"

"Hm? Oh." Paul pushed and turned the slate toward Luis so he could read it. "It's Durbin. I have some people keeping an eye on him and sending me reports. After what happened back on Earth I fully expect him to get up to something… questionable. At best."

"And what have you found so far?"

"He seems to be trying to build a coalition of some kind. Lots of individual meetings, and hanging out with Stokes and his little group."

"Sounds like he's campaigning…"

"Maybe. But I can almost guarantee it's more than that. There's been the suggestion that some strong-arming is going on."

"But no proof yet?"

"No. Not yet. My people haven't seen anything directly."

"So…"

"No, you don't understand. Durbin practically destroyed two families to get himself appointed as a Mission Commander." Paul held his hand up, "And before you ask—no, I cannot **prove** that, but I am **convinced** that's what happened. He almost derailed the mission altogether, just to gain himself a little more power."

Luis opened his mouth to speak, but Paul barreled on.

"He's planning something, Luis, and I will not let him jeopardize the colony. We've worked too hard to make this happen, and these people are counting on us—now more than ever."

"Can you hear yourself? This thing with Durbin is getting out of hand. We need to focus on what's really important— getting the colony bootstrapped and on its own feet. Have some faith in the people who chose—who **we** chose—to be here. If you can't trust Durbin, trust **them**."

"I **did** trust them!" Paul took a breath. "**Do** trust them. But Luis, things are different now. We can't afford to just trust that things will work out. We can't leave this to chance… or to trust. The only way this will work is if we **make** it work."

"Then you had better get back to **that**." Luis stood and

stepped towards Paul's desk. "Forget Durbin—it won't matter who runs the council if the colony itself can't survive." He turned and walked toward the door.

At the threshold, he turned back to say, "Let it go, Paul," before he continued into the hallway.

EXCHANGE

"LET'S GET THIS CYCLER CLOSED UP," LEANA SAID AS SHE dropped her wrench into the toolbox.

Ten air cyclers were situated around the dome's perimeter about six hundred meters apart, three of which she and Alice had brought online so far this morning.

Leana stood and brushed at the powdery dust that coated her knees. It was a pointless act—her entire suit had taken on a reddish-orange tint, especially around the joints and creases where even the airlocks' electrostatic "scrubbers" couldn't dislodge the dust. *Should have just made the damned suits orange*, she thought. *Maybe I'll update the program for the next batch.*

"I'm no geophysics expert," Alice said as she latched the cycler's panel, "but I'm thinking the Earth is screwed."

"Alice…"

Since Luis had broken the news of Earth's possible ejection from the solar system, many had expressed similar thoughts. Though the colonists had been vetted and selected for psychological stability, the nature and scope of the recent tragedy had left many in a fragile state. *Under extraordinary pressure, even the strongest stone will break.*

An unfortunate few had fallen into self-destructive behaviors, hopelessness, or—*like Alice*—cynicism. Leana struggled with some of this herself, even as she helped others do the same.

Alice hadn't yet come to her for counseling, but sometimes working closely with someone afforded some less formal opportunities.

"What? It's true, right?" Alice closed and picked up the toolbox. "They're spinning off into oblivion and there's nothing we can do to stop it or help them." She gestured with her free arm as she spoke.

"That may be true, but you could be a bit more… respectful about it."

"I guess," Alice replied. "Just don't see the point, I guess. No sense being all sentimental about it… better to accept it and move on. Sure, it's tragic, but that doesn't mean I have to lie in my bunk and cry about it."

"It's easier to think of them as already gone. Easier to cover your grief in a blanket of cynical distancing." Leana stepped closer to Alice to look her in the eyes. "You deal with it however you need to, of course, as long as you remember there are others grieving who might be in a more sensitive place. Not everyone will find your attitude acceptable, or welcome."

"Who else am I going to talk to about it, Lee?" Alice looked away. "Besides, I know *you* can handle it. You are our resident shrink, after all."

"Do you? Perhaps. Nevertheless, try to be considerate. As the 'resident shrink,' the last thing I need is you running around upsetting people."

"You got it, boss." Alice met her eyes again.

Leana held the look for a moment. "Hm." She glanced down the dome wall. "Now, let's head to number four… see if we can get *it* online too before we call it a day."

The dome stretched overhead as far as Leana could see,

and she fought the urge to take off her helmet in the enclosed space. The interlocking geodesics swam in her vision and she fought an unexpected wave of nausea. *Oookay… don't look up, I guess.* If that was going to keep happening, she'd have to slap an anti-nausea patch on the next time she suited up. *What the hell is going on with me lately?*

Her boots kicked up plumes of ruddy dust, and she wondered how the green lake's humidity—once fully established—would affect the Martian regolith.

Even with the shell incomplete, the average temperatures inside the dome had stabilized just above zero and the ice had started to melt. They'd need to move quickly to get the dome closed up and pressurized before the ice sublimated.

Once the cyclers were operational, they would circulate the air and maintain an elevated pressure inside the dome—not Earth normal, but above Mars' average and high enough to keep the water from boiling off. Eventually, clouds would obscure the dome's distant top, suspended in thin, but breathable air. It would be nice to see an Earth-like climate again, *even if I do still have to wear a pressure suit to enjoy it.*

Leana looked out across the crater and the empty expanse somehow felt more vast than that between Earth and Mars. She shuffled closer to Alice as they walked, and fixed her eyes on the number four cycler, still fifty meters away.

"I LOVE THIS PLACE," Leana said of the view outside the personal transport's faceted, wraparound window. "Reminds me of the desert, back home. When Luis and I were scouting the crater, something about this spot hit me just the right way." She pulled a small wine bottle and a couple of glasses from a crate. "Here." She handed Sheila a glass.

In the distance, the crater's rim divided the fading sunlight from the encroaching darkness. Tendrils of light from the colony reached across the crater toward them and the enormous, partially completed dome that rose into the Martian twilight a few dozen meters to the north. Work lights glinted off the dome as her team and their automated carts hauled exterior panels up its side like a colony of ants.

"I brought this with us two years ago," she said as she peeled the foil from the bottle, "because I knew I'd be missing you and would want an excuse to drag you out to celebrate when you got here." She pulled the cork and poured wine into each of their glasses. "Sorry it's taken us so long to get out here."

"There's been a lot going on." Sheila rolled the wine around in her glass. She sniffed at the rim lightly and nodded. "Mmm, very nice. It weathered the trip well."

Leana raised her glass. "I... don't even know what to toast."

"To old friends, then," Sheila said.

"And bold adventures." Leana completed their traditional toast, and they clinked glasses. "Cheers."

The wine at her nose had all the right notes, but something about it turned her stomach. She took a small sip and felt her throat constrict as a cold flush rose from her chest to the top of her head. *Okay, that's not right.* Nausea, again.

"Lee, you okay?"

"Yeah, I'm just..." she placed the back of her hand to her forehead, which felt cold and wet with perspiration. She sat her glass down and reviewed her mental calendar. *Five, six days?* She'd have to consult her AI when she got home. "I'm fine. Probably just overworked."

Sheila sipped the wine as twilight faded into dusk and the few visible stars twinkled weakly through the haze. Leana left her glass unfinished as they sank into a comfortable moment of silence.

"The dome is an impressive sight already," Sheila said. "I'm amazed how quickly it's going up!"

"Luis and I have been pulling parts from the compositor for months in preparation, but the whole team has busted their asses to assemble them. It's a gruesome schedule, but they're motivated. My first shifters are one of the most cohesive, cooperative teams I've ever worked with."

"You used to having so many people underfoot yet?"

Leana laughed. "It was weird the first day or so, but y'know… pretty much haven't had time to even think about it since then."

"Yeah."

"So how 'bout you? Settling in okay?"

"Oh, yeah," Sheila said. "We've got the few things we brought with us out of the storage containers, and my lab was already partially set up—thanks for that, by the way—so I've just been pulling smaller parts to get the basic equipment finished and functional. There's not been a big push for Biomedical Engineering services yet, thankfully, but it's only a matter of time before somebody falls down a crater wall or off your oversized geodesic monkey bars out there and breaks something. Until then, I'm looking forward to ramping up my research. In fact, I'm driving out to The Cradle tomorrow to secure a few samples."

Sheila poured herself a second glass of wine. It was too dark outside now to see much beyond the colony's light, except for the dome that seemed to undulate under the moving work lights.

Sheila seemed to wrestle with something she wanted to share. Over the course of their friendship, Leana had witnessed a hundred variations of that struggle. Her friend's eyes glistened with tears.

"Oh, Lee, what are we gonna do?" Sheila blurted. "My family is gone. Our entire history is gone. Everything we ever dreamed of or loved or worked for is gone. Honestly, I don't know if I want to keep going, or to program one of those rovers out there to dig a hole and push me in."

"Sheila," Leana said. "We are going to do what we **have** to do. The Earth may be gone, and our friends and families with her, but that doesn't mean we've lost them. We have what we keep with us, in us. Our dreams and everything we've worked for are **here**. Our hope is **here**. Our future is **here**. I knew before I left that I would probably never see Earth again. I knew that everyone I knew would grow old and die and that I wouldn't be able to share that with them. The only thing we've lost is the slim chance we might ever go back, and we're left with the knowledge that their hopes and dreams and futures were cut short." Leana reached out to hold her friend's hand. "But our future is still ahead of us. What we do **now** is live. We fill this world with life. We keep their memory—and our history—for future generations." She let go and refilled Sheila's glass. "Now, drink this wine, and let's talk about our future."

DEDICATION

Leana stood before the crowd of pressure-suited colonists here at the base of the greenhouse crater to dedicate the dome and the green lake within. The dome rose and curved away high above them from the lip of the crater which itself stood some six meters high.

Paul and Charles stood beside her under the pretense of their status as Mission Commanders, though it seemed clear to Leana that they were there more as a campaign stunt to glad-hand and promote themselves than to actually celebrate the colony's achievement. Charles waved to the crowd while Paul shuffled nervously, and Leana tried—discretely—to move farther away.

Politics was distastefully self-righteous, and she only paid as much attention to it as she had to. Her and Luis' chief concern had always been the kids and the world they would inherit, which had generally led them toward shared goals, though they still occasionally locked horns over specific measures or points of policy that they thought would bring the best results.

Ultimately, their shared goals had brought them to this inhospitable, dust-ridden planet and the dream of a future haven—not just for themselves and the boys, but for humanity. Collectively, humanity had only barely pulled itself from the brink of sociological and ecological self-destruction, and had, in the process, gained knowledge they would use here to establish a new home for the species.

The boys would inherit a new world, and a have a guaranteed place in it. They would be free to pursue almost any vocation, and the colony would benefit exponentially more, and more directly, from their contributions than the Earth ever would have. They would inhabit a world that they would build themselves, literally, from the ground up.

The beginning of that world stood behind her now, embodied in the massive structure her teams had nearly completed.

"Lee," Paul addressed her over their suits' proximity mesh channel, "congratulations on this unprecedented accomplishment."

He'd never worn politics well, and his smarmy posturing now rendered him practically a stranger.

"Thanks," she said.

"Yes," Durbin said, "it's amazing what we can accomplish with the right motivation."

"And what about you, Charles?" Paul asked. "Manufactured any good conspiracies lately?"

"Paul, please," Leana said, "now is not the time."

"Of course," Paul replied, holding up both hands toward her, "Won't happen again."

Leana stepped forward and activated the open broadcast channel to address both the assembled crowd—mostly first- and second-shifters in their overlap period—and the rest of the colony. A video feed was also available, which one of her first-shifters had been tasked to provide from their helmet cam, so everyone could view or listen as they were able.

A small mixed-shift crew stood atop the crater wall a few

meters above and behind her, ready with the final triangular panel that would—at least ceremonially—complete the two-kilometer geodesic dome.

"Today is a momentous day," Leana began. "Today we honor our colony's first major collective achievement, which, thanks to your tireless dedication, we're celebrating almost four weeks ahead of schedule! You should all be proud of what you've accomplished, as I am of you." Leana continued, "This massive dome is a testament to your hard work, and represents the future of this colony. The green lake it makes possible—the first stable body of water on Mars in almost four billion years! —will soon supply enough food and oxygen to sustain us and drive the cultivation of this world. With its completion, we have taken the first step towards transforming Mars into a vibrant new home for humanity."

Leana gestured to her team, who lifted the translucent panel into position and secured it in place.

"In appreciation of this accomplishment," Leana continued, "in thanks to those who've volunteered their time and their energy, and in honor of our former home, we proudly dedicate this installation to Earth's memory and to our Martian future, with the name: 'Lake Hope.'"

Some in the crowd clapped gloved hands, while others toggled their locator beacons on and off, which blinked their exterior lights and sent an audible chirp over the open channel in an electronic approximation of the gesture.

A sense of unity around their common achievement seemed to prevail, but then Paul and Charles waded into the crowd, which fractured and pooled around them.

Leana sighed. *I guess some things will never change.*

FAREWELL

As Luis strode down the hallway toward Paul's office, the energy recovery system under the floor cushioned his footfalls. It was one of those sensations he forgot to notice until he stepped a certain way.

He pressed the activation panel when he reached the door, which immediately slid open. He entered, a half-smirk on his face.

"What?" Paul seemed to be in a dark mood.

"What, what?"

"What's with the face?"

"Oh, uh…" Luis chuckled, "I ran into Lily Simmons on the way over."

"Who?"

"Oh, uh, Lily Lancaster. She and Simon weren't even dating when Leana and I left. I'm still adjusting to the name change."

"And?"

"Well, she's expecting." Luis grinned and took a seat in the chair in front of Paul's desk.

"That was fast."

"It seems she and Simon made the most of their off-shift time on the flight over."

"Well, good for them," Paul said. "We've been needing some good news around here."

"You say that," Luis said, "but *you* look like you need something more than good news. Election not going well?"

"How long have we known each other, Luis?"

Luis shifted in his seat. "Long enough to know that a question like that predicates a conversation I'm not going to like."

"Fair enough," Paul said.

Luis sighed. "Just spit it out, Paul."

"Right," Paul said. "So I've discovered something... something troubling about Durbin."

"Lots of things about Durbin are troubling."

"Just... watch this," Paul turned his display toward Luis and started a video that was apparently of a meeting between Durbin and five of his buddies.

Luis furrowed his brow and shot Paul a look. "What is this?"

"Keep watching," Paul said.

In video after video, Durbin and his allies either plotted to undermine the election directly, or pressured other colonists to cast their votes for him. They preyed on the colonists' lingering fears, and if that didn't work, resorted to mental and physical intimidation.

The videos were from all over the colony, in both public and private spaces.

*How does he **have** these videos? It shouldn't be possible.*

In one, a group—gathered outside in their suits at night—performed some sort of ceremony or ritual. Helmet cam footage followed several people as they pulled the mission patch from their suits and dropped them into a flaming bowl as they chanted something about "Mother Mars."

There's no way he should have these recordings.

In another, Tony Madia and Durbin huddled in some small room in the central pod, with Tony hunched over a slate that appeared to be patched into data lines.

Paul leaned toward Luis and whispered, "I was also in the system during this one, setting up roadblocks as they tried to get through…"

Tony tapped feverishly while Durbin harangued and berated him over his apparent inability to alter the voting algorithms in Charles' favor.

After this final recording, the display faded to black and Paul turned the screen back around.

Luis pressed the bridge of his nose and clenched his jaw. "Well," he said, "this is… disturbing."

There was so much was wrong with all of this that he struggled to find a response. Paul waited quietly.

It took Luis an uncomfortably long time to find the right tack, but finally he spoke.

"Obviously, we have to do something about Durbin and his friends. Even if you stopped their direct attempts to rig the election, we can't allow the intimidation and bullying. We'll have to present this to the council when the election is over."

"It's not just the election rigging," Paul interrupted. "This 'Mother Mars' stuff is unsettling, and it seems like Durbin has slithered his way right into the middle of it."

"I assume… I **hope,**" Luis gently tapped the top of the desk for emphasis, "that the reason you have these recordings is because someone reported Durbin's activity to you. That someone gave you a reason to watch him?" He paused only a moment for a centering breath before he continued. "But… there are other aspects of this that concern me."

Luis struggled to put his thoughts into words.

"First, why didn't you come to me as soon as you heard what was going on? Why keep me out of the loop on this?" Another pause, another breath. "But my biggest concern is that the earliest of these recordings appear to be **before** they'd actually done anything. How were you even able to **get** those recordings? **I** set these systems up myself—we only store video for a few hours unless there's an environmental or security alert. You couldn't have retrieved these after the fact."

Luis knew Paul well enough to see an inner conflict play across his face. Apparently, he'd expected a different reaction. Luis' ears grew hot and his breath short. *Centering be damned.*

"Paul," Luis said, as gently as he could manage, "please tell me someone tipped you off about Charles' plans."

"I…" Paul glanced down at his hands, folded in his lap, "can't tell you that."

"Damnit, Paul." The heat drained out of him.

"Look," Paul started. "We both know what kind of person Durbin is. We've both seen how he's reacted to this… situation." He stood and stepped toward the corner of his desk. "Durbin has it in his head that we—that you and I—are more interested in holding onto power than we are in a stable and productive colony."

"And now you've gone and proven him right."

"No!" Paul slammed his hand on his desk and thrust a finger in Luis' direction. "We talked about this!" A thread of desperation found root in Paul's voice. "Charles Durbin is a danger to this colony. My only interest is in protecting it, and preserving what's left of the human race! We've lost too much already. Too much! We can't let him jeopardize our future and risk everything we have left to lose."

"You're right. We can't let this pass." Luis stood and stepped toward the door. "But it seems you've already lost more than you realize." He turned back to face Paul. "This was supposed to be a new chapter for humanity, a new opportunity, a chance to **be better**. But now you've compromised those principles. You can't control everything, and now you've lost control of yourself. Instead of holding Durbin to the higher standards of this colony, you've lowered yourself to his. The Paul I built this project with would never have allowed this."

"You're wrong. Everything has changed, and I've only done what's best for the colony."

"No. You've done what **_you think_** is best for the colony," Luis replied. "I am going to present this to the council, and it'll be up to them to determine whether you're right."

Two YEARS of regular use had smoothed the path between the Central Pod and HAB 1, and Luis' individual transport seemed to glide on its semi-rigid wheels across the compacted Martian dust. Between Phobos' dim light, the incidental light of the colony, and his transport's headlamp, he could just make out the bounds of the path. The transport's sensors would guide him around anything too dark or small to see that might lie ahead.

"Fucking Paul." Luis muttered. He'd played out the thing with Paul over and over in his head while he tried to focus and wrap up his day. *What had he expected? That I would just go along with it?*

His AI chimed an error tone in his helmet.

"Sorry," he reacted, "Uh, any election results to report?"

There are currently eleven locked responses, the computer replied. *Paul Robinson currently leads with a clear majority, but there are not yet enough locked votes to project the outcome. However, if current trends hold, reasonable projections may be possible with as few as fifty responses.*

"Well, keep me apprised."

Luis hadn't seen Leana or the kids since morning, and though he **should** be excited to get home to them, Paul's revelations had set this day into a lengthening string of difficult days and meant an uncomfortable conversation when he got home.

The idea that Paul assumed Luis would understand—*even sanction!*—his actions made Luis crazy. He wasn't one to avoid hard decisions, but now he couldn't—in good conscience—vote for Paul.

Hopefully, whomever the colony chose would learn to act responsibly under the yoke of actual leadership. If the colony allowed them to remain in office once he told them what the two of them had done.

If I tell them what they've done.

He needed to talk to Leana. She'd know what to do. Should he tell the colony and throw everything into chaos, or let things move forward, get all the cards on the table, and sort everything out later?

He could have put in his own name of course, and probably would have done well, but he was here to build a home and a family, and didn't have the taste for politics and administration. He knew he could make a difference on the council, so he'd serve if asked, but he'd be just as happy to leave all of that to others.

Leana would be a great Chief Councilor, but, selfishly, he didn't want to give up any more time with her. The past two years had been exhausting for both of them, and it would be nice to have more opportunities to enjoy just being with each other again.

Luis wasn't sure how Leana would handle what he had to tell her. Paul had always been more her friend than his.

The computer chimed Leana's comms tone in his ear. "Hi, sweetie," he said.

"Long day?"

"Has there been any other kind, lately?"

"Ugh, true. **But**, we got the last of the cyclers online today and seeded the lake with algae, which should take hold over the next several days as temps stabilize."

"That's great, sweetie."

"Uh huh. Is something bothering you beyond your 'long day'?" she asked.

"Yeah, but look, I'm two minutes out. I'll talk to you about it at home." The general message tone chimed. "And I just got a ping, sweetie. I'll see you shortly."

He ended the connection after her reply, and acknowledged the computer.

"Go ahead."

Several monitoring stations are reporting abnormal readings and I have an updated election report for you.

"Details."

Atmospheric monitors report increases in pressure and H_2O concentration. Multiple stations and orbital monitors have confirmed. Mobile drilling stations K7 and C9 report H_2O in stable cold liquid pressure and temperature regimes, against predictive models and logged surveys.

They'd expected changes in atmospheric conditions, but if the drilling stations had discovered liquid water... well, that was huge. The geo team would have to go check it out first thing in the morning.

Election results continue to show Paul Robinson with a narrowing lead for Chief Councillor.

Luis pulled his two-wheeled transport to a stop near HAB 1, activated its automated self-docking into the HAB's charging compartment, then climbed the steps to enter the airlock.

"Continue monitoring atmospherics and report significant changes," Luis said. "And you said Paul's lead is narrowing. Who is his top challenger?"

Current rankings show Paul Robinson leading Luis Pendrova by fewer than ten points. Other nominees trail sufficiently to predict their elimination.

Me? Luis froze, momentarily stunned. *What the hell?*

"Who nominated me? And when? I wasn't on the ballot, last I checked."

Leana Pendrova, at 0745 this morning.

"Damnit, Lee."

He placed his pressure suit and helmet into the decon alcove, where targeted ultrasonics, electrostatics, and puffs of air dislodged the dust while negative pressure whisked it away.

Luis opened the inner door and entered his home.

"Daddy, daddy!" Gabriel, in his hand-me-down PJs, rushed to him and latched onto his leg as he stepped across the airlock threshold into their living area. Michael sauntered along behind his brother, dressed in the simple gray PJs produced by the colony's compositor. Both boys had outgrown all the clothes they'd brought with them, though some of Michael's had simply migrated to his younger brother.

"Sorry, honey," Leana said from the kitchen, "they insisted on staying up til you got home."

"Well, then I'm sorry it took me so long. You boys should be in bed!" Luis picked Gabriel up and tousled Michael's hair, which was still damp from the shower. "Did you have fun at school today?"

"Yeah! Yeah!" Gabriel clapped his hands together. "We had an election!"

"Oh, really?" Luis asked, "an election for what?"

"An election!" Gabriel shouted.

"For council leader," Michael clarified.

"Ah, I see. And were either of you nominated?" Luis set Gabriel down and continued down the steps into the living room.

"No, daddy, Mrs. Greenwood let us vote in the real election!" Gabriel said.

"Oh, really. So, did Mr. Robinson or Mr. Durbin win the election?"

"You did Daddy!" Gabriel said.

"I di…" Luis shot a look in Leana's direction, and she raised her eyebrows and shrugged her shoulders. "But I wasn't nominated," Luis said. "How did I win?"

Gabriel looked up at Michael, who stared at his shoes.

"I…" Michael paused, "I asked Mrs. Greenwood if we could nominate someone else."

"You asked Mrs. Greenwood? What made you think to ask that?"

"I was talking with Nanny about the election—the real election—before school this morning, and asked why you weren't a… candidate," Michael said. "She said that no one had nominated you. I asked if someone could vote for you anyway, and she said someone would have to nominate you, or that people could just decide to vote for you without you being nominated at all."

"Really," Luis said. "Nanny told you all that?"

"Yeah, so, I thought that if I just voted for you, maybe no one else would know they could too, but if I nominated you, then everybody would know, and you might win!" Michael grinned.

"And you did win, Daddy!" Gabriel added.

"Only our election, Gabes, not the real one." Michael looked from Gabriel to Luis. "I've tried to explain it to him, Daddy, but he doesn't understand."

"That's ok, Michael, he's still a bit too little."

"I am not little!" Gabriel pouted and stomped over to his chair next to the couch.

Luis took the opportunity to step back up into the kitchen and kiss Leana. He held her for a moment, then took her hand and led her to the couch. He sat and pulled her down beside him.

"But, as it turns out," Luis said as he put his arms around her, "*someone* **did** nominate me for the real election."

"I know, Daddy, Michael did!" Gabriel said. "After we got

home, Michael told Nanny all about the election at school, and he told her that you should be… nominated, since all the kids voted for you. Then Nanny said that you were nominated!"

"Boys," Leana intertwined her fingers with Luis', "you've gotten to see Daddy. Now please go get in your beds—I'll be there to tuck you in in a few minutes."

"Yes, Mommy," both boys replied.

Gabriel ran up to Luis and snuggled briefly inside his free arm, and Luis wrapped him in a hug. "Goodnight Daddy," Gabriel said, and kissed his cheek.

"G'night Gabes," Luis said. "Hasta Mañana."

"Goodnight, Michael," Luis called after Michael, who was already halfway down the hall.

"Goodnight, Daddy!"

Leana snuggled up closer. For a moment, cinnamon and lavender enveloped him, and everything was silent except for the sounds of their boys as they played and settled into their beds.

The general message tone chimed in the air between them, and he looked at her as he responded. "Go ahead."

Now projecting Durbin loss, with 137 locked responses. If current percentages hold, additional projections may not be possible until voting has concluded.

"Explain."

Current locked responses break down as follows: Paul Robinson: fifty-five, Luis Pendrova: fifty-two, Leana Pendrova: fifteen, the remaining candidates have insufficient first and second choice votes to progress beyond the first runoff round.

"Okay. Thank you."

"I… kind of have a confession to make," Leana said.

"I thought you might."

"I've been talking to people on the Greenhouse teams," Leana said, "and most of them aren't happy with how Paul and Durbin have been handling this whole thing. Then

Michael mentioned his conversation with Nanny this morning, and, well, I nominated you. I'm sorry I didn't tell you… we've both been so busy."

"But… why?"

"Paul and Durbin have both been acting like politicians—like children—taking petty little shots at each other. At this point, I don't think either of them deserves to win."

"But… why me?" Luis asked. "I mean, you know how I feel about it. We've talked about this. I don't want to be a politician, I don't want to be an administrator. I want to build this colony, I want to make this place a home. I don't want to make it a… job."

"The people trust you. I trust you," Leana said. "So, what will you do?"

"If I win?"

"What will you do if you win?"

"I'll take the job, I guess," Luis said. "Because if the people want me, who am I to tell them no? And… there are other reasons."

Leana looked puzzled, but waited for him to continue.

"Ok, look, I know Paul is a friend—hell, you've trusted him longer than you've known me," Luis said. "But I think everything that's happened has affected him more than he's letting on. You said it yourself, he's been acting like an idiot."

Leana sat up a bit to face him more fully, and her confused expression darkened into concern.

"Paul showed me something today," Luis began, "that implicates Durbin in some serious criminal activity… well, criminal on Earth, anyway. Durbin and his supporters have coerced and bullied people, and tried to hack the AI to favor him in the election. He might have succeeded if Paul hadn't stopped him. But Paul only knew to stop him because he'd abused his authority and access to make the AI record and store everything Durbin and his people said and did since nominations were opened. And he did it before Durbin or his people had even done anything wrong, just because he suspected they **might** do something wrong."

"Oh my god," Leana said.

"So, you're right—they're both compromised," Luis said. "I've been over it and over it. I should have halted the election this morning as soon as Paul told me. I should have told the whole colony what they've both done—gotten it out in the open. I'm still not entirely sure why I haven't." He pressed the heels of his hands against his temples, then gritted his teeth and growled quietly as he ran both hands roughly through his hair.

"The problem," he continued, "is that Paul Robinson is… or was… the only person who's really qualified for the job—the only one with the leadership experience to take us through the transition from scientists and mission specialists to a functioning civil community."

"I don't even know what to say…" Leana started, "Paul… I mean, I knew something was going on, but I never imagined he was capable of compromising himself this way. He must have had some reason…"

"No, he didn't," Luis interrupted. "He just assumed Durbin would try something and decided to spy on him, instead of bringing his concerns to us." Luis took her hand in his and caressed it. "So this is why, as upset as I may be about you nominating me for this stupid position, if it falls to me, I'll have no choice but to take it," Luis said. "I'm not the most qualified and I don't want it, but there's no one else I would trust to do it… apart from you, of course."

Luis pulled her close again and wrapped both arms around her. Now that he'd gotten it off his chest, his frustration subsided to a tiny buzz at the back of his head.

Everything melted away when he was close to her. He closed his eyes and descended into her spicy, floral scent, which mixed with the barely perceptible tang of sweat, and the ever-present rust of martian dust.

The corners of his mouth raised into a slight smile and he opened his eyes. "You better go tuck the boys in," he said. "Then come find me. I need to show you how much I missed you today."

She flashed him a mischievous smile of her own, and he watched her walk back to the boys' room. Even after a day out in a suit on the surface, she was damn sexy. *Don't know how she does it, but she always manages to look sexy, whatever she's doing.* Today though it was something more—she practically glowed. Maybe he just needed to be close to her again. Whatever it was, he wanted her, and he'd make sure she knew it.

A chime sounded near his left ear.

Voting has concluded, the computer intoned over the focused audio. *The results are as follows: with seventy-three of one hundred forty-four votes cast, Paul Robinson has been elected as Chief Councillor by runoff against Luis Pendrova with seventy-one votes. Council representatives are: Luis Pendrova, Leana Pendrova, Susan Lancaster, Charles Durbin, and Eileen Dydo.*

Well, there ya go, Luis thought. *Now, I've got more important things to do.* He walked toward their bedroom with a relaxed smile.

FLEE

LEANA SAT ON A BENCH IN THE HALL OUTSIDE THE CENTRAL Pod's main airlocks and skimmed her patients' daily logs as she waited for Sheila to arrive. Skim was all she could manage. Her thoughts jumbled scattershot after last night's revelations, the election, and this morning's checkup with the new doctor.

The doctor—who had pulled rank to coerce her to go for a checkup—had voiced the same suspicions about Leana's recurring nausea and other symptoms that Leana herself had been quietly agonizing over. *But it's too early yet to tell, and there's too much else to worry about. Won't do any good to get all worked up over a possibility.*

The logs she was too distracted to read held little of interest beyond the usual petty domestic complaints, minor paranoias, disturbing dreams, election-related rants, or a kind of breathless reverence for Mars. Despite her encouragements, very few dealt in any direct way with Earth's (and their) tragedy. It seemed most, like herself, were still using work and colony drama to avoid a confrontation with deeper issues.

She got it. She'd already composed an election rant or two of her own—in her head—especially after she'd learned what

Paul had done. *I should probably talk to someone*, she thought. *Too bad I'm the colony's only psychiatrist.*

Leana jumped as the southwest airlock opened, and someone fell through it into the hallway. A second person followed them through.

"Keep moving, ya bastard." The second person grabbed the first by their pressure suit's helmet collar.

These were followed by two others who dragged a fifth—bruised, bloodied, and unconscious—through the opening. Leana stood and approached before they could turn down the corridor into the building.

"What the hell is going on here?"

Tyler Leeds turned toward her and she had a moment of confusion.

"Oh, Dr. Pendrova, sorry," Tyler replied. "These two attacked Chuck Dabney, and Dr. Robinson told us they've been threatening a bunch of people. Apparently, they'd tried to intimidate people into voting for Durbin, then after he lost they decided to make good on their threats."

"So, you had to beat them to a pulp?"

"Well, Tony didn't put up much of a fight, but Peter here…" Tyler grunted as he lifted Peter slightly, as though to give her a better look, "apparently he was an amateur middleweight champ before the CNSEA brought him on board. It took all three of us to take him down."

"Well, you should have been more careful, it looks like one of his patches got ripped off. His suit could have been compromised."

"We didn't do that," Tyler replied. "He wasn't **that** much trouble. Several of Durbin's other goons have been walking around with missing patches. I think it's part of that 'Mother Mars' cult stuff."

"The what now?" Leana made a mental note to look a little more closely at her logs.

"I don't really know, for sure. Just rumors, mainly."

"Well, just make sure his suit goes to reclamation. Then when everything settles down, I want all of you to stop by my office for a chat."

"Yes ma'am."

The group trudged off down the hallway, with Peter slung between them. Sure enough, Tony was missing the same patch on his suit. *Definitely not a coincidence. What the hell is going on?*

The comms system chimed in her ear just as a transport engaged the east airlock behind her, and the unmistakable *chunk-chunk-hsss* of grapples and pressurization came through the bulkheads and the floor as much as through the door. Composited from native materials, the building was sturdy and airtight, but hardly soundproof.

"Yes?"

"Dr. Pendrova? I have preliminary results from your blood test."

Already? "Go ahead."

"It's still quite early, but everything I'm seeing says that congratulations are in order! You are definitely pregnant."

The airlock door opened and Sheila Robinson stepped out, smiled, and rushed to hug her.

"Lee!" Sheila shouted.

"Dr. Pendrova?" The doctor said in her ear.

Leana held a finger up to Sheila, who was practically bouncing.

"Yes, I understand. Thank you."

Pregnant! She reeled momentarily, but Sheila didn't seem to notice.

After two years with Luis and the boys, Leana had forgotten how weird other people could be, especially "Morning Sheila."

"Did you hear?" Sheila smiled so big it made Leana's cheeks hurt. "Of course you heard!" She wrapped Leana in an uncomfortably tight hug. "Oh my gosh, it's so exciting! What a race! You almost pulled it off, too! Luis did really, really well, but Paul just managed to squeak it out at the end."

"Yeah, of course, I'm..." *What am I? Happy? Angry? In shock, probably.*

"Of course, we're going to have a celebratory dinner! You and Luis are obviously invited... unless you don't want to come... but you have to come! There's so much to do!"

"Shei..."

"I'm going to see Paul right now. He's been here since 0400, getting an early start—you know how he is," Sheila said, and headed down the corridor.

"Sheila." Leana's tone brought her friend to a stop. "I'm very happy for Paul, there's no one..." she wrestled with her contempt and realized she still had no idea how she should handle this, "...better suited to the job than him. Luis didn't even want to be nominated." She continued in a feigned whisper, "He's still a bit sore at me about that."

"You never told him!" Sheila laughed and resumed her progress toward Paul's office. "I would love to have seen the look on his face when you told him. It'll take him days to get over that, I bet."

"Not really," Leana struggled to catch up. "There are more important things going on right now." *Like the fact that your husband betrayed our trust.*

They stopped at the intersection where the cross corridor lead to Leana's office in one direction, and to Paul's in the other.

"Look," Leana caught Sheila's elbow. "There is something I need to talk to you about. Paul..."

"The last few days have been hard on everybody," Sheila interrupted. "We'll all feel better once things settle down. If there's one thing a crap-ton of scientists and engineers are good at, it's staying focused..." She trailed off as the sound of someone running reverberated through the structure. They shared a confused look as Stephen Miers careened into the corridor behind them.

"Water!" He said, breathless. "Filling the crater!" He ran past them and on to the next corridor. Sheila's eyes went wide.

"Let's go," Leana said.

LEANA AND SHEILA followed close behind Miers who sprinted towards Luis' office.

"Sensors!" He panted as he practically burst through the door. "South crater wall. Water!"

Leana and Sheila entered directly behind him.

"Slow down and take a breath," Luis said. "What's going on?"

"We got alerts from several stations along the southern wall." Stephen struggled to catch his breath. "It's not *traces* of water they're detecting anymore—it's *liquid* water. On the surface!"

"What?"

"Subsurface temps have risen enough that the ice is melting, and atmospheric pressures are high enough that the water isn't immediately sublimating, but the resulting water is almost certainly boiling. Two of the stations appear to be partially submerged. Our drones show that part of the crater wall has collapsed, and the water is rising, fast. At this rate, it will reach us in less than thirty minutes."

Luis stood. "Get back to your team and get me some recommendations—can we get to higher ground?" He paused expectantly, but Miers seemed held in place, so he shouted, "Go!"

Leana's chest solidified and her face went cold as the implications of Miers' report sunk in. She took a step toward Luis, whose face only betrayed a quiet determination. She knew enough, though, to recognize his position—hands on his desk, elbows locked, his eyes focused on some infinite point—which told her he was fully engaged with this new problem.

"Leana, can we get the maintenance boats out of the lake greenhouse in time?"

"Maybe," Leana said, "but they're not finished yet."

"Will they float?"

"The hulls are complete, so yeah, they should."

"Good enough. Have whoever is at the dome prep for evacuation and recovery. They're to launch as soon as it's safe after the water gets here. Two people per boat, comms to emergency frequencies. The rest of the colony should get to crew transports if possible, or find a safe space in the HABs. We'll communicate a rally point and further instructions as soon as Miers' team has it," Luis said. "Sheila, tell Paul to meet me in Comms—we've got to try to secure the remote equipment—then get everyone in the building to the center, away from the outer walls."

Sheila sprinted from the room, and Luis walked around his desk to Leana. He reached up and caressed her face, and, for just a moment, everything else fell away.

"You should go to the center with the others. It should be safer there," Luis said. Sheila's emergency message rang out loudly in the room, but he ignored it and pulled Leana close. "But I want you near me. Is that selfish of me?"

"Yes." Leana brought her mouth within centimeters of his ear. "But I'm coming with you anyway." He tightened around her as she kissed his cheek and they lost themselves in the moment.

They left the office together and ran toward the communications room. As they ran, Leana called out instructions first to her team to prep the boats, then to the colony at large to batten the hatches. Tamra practically ran into them on her way to the

Comms room, and Paul also rushed down the corridor toward them.

"What the hell is going on, Luis?" Paul shouted.

"You know about as much as I do."

"You have a plan?"

"Something resembling a plan, anyway. Not sure it'll work, but we have to try."

Luis talked them through it as they rushed ahead.

Dust seals on the colony's equipment should also serve—at least for a short time—to keep out water. Autonomous rovers and other remotely operable machines might not float, but hopefully they would be buoyant enough not to sink into the crater floor as it turned to mud. The larger transports should certainly float, and, like the rovers, had wheels with retractable flaps for use in soft sands, which should work like paddles in the water. And, because all the wheels had independent motors, they should not only be able to propel the vehicles in water, but also to steer them.

All the HABs and the Central Pod sat on low supports, but were not anchored to them or the ground, so they should float if the water rose high enough. The biggest question was structural integrity. Individual rooms—or whole sections—could be sealed off if the buildings' exteriors were breached, so if everyone moved to the center, they should be safe. Once afloat, the boats and transports could latch onto exterior hard points and tug them to higher ground.

"Well," Paul said, "all we can do is try."

The computer beeped in Luis' ear.

"Dr. Pendrova, it's Miers. The northwest escarpment is our best bet. Rover traffic there has already compacted a path up and out of the crater, which should be stable and high enough to get us above the water. The slope is gentle enough to climb on foot if necessary, and the transports can handle it easily."

"Thanks, Stephen. Now get your people to the central offices."

"We're already moving."

Luis transmitted the rendezvous coordinates to all transports, then he, Tamra, and Paul input instructions to reprogram and recall the rovers and other mobile equipment. Leana filled the colony in on the plan and directed any occupied crew transports to attach to the nearest occupied habitat.

Reports streamed in from individuals and crews who had been working out in the crater as they reached the escarpment.

For fifteen minutes, the four of them worked to ensure they'd accounted for everyone, and that they were as ready as they could be.

"Erratic wheel rotation and stabilization reports coming in from almost every mobile unit," Paul said. "The readings are consistent with what I would expect from drive systems in water."

Outside between the window in the rear wall and the far northern crater wall, the dry desert view to which Leana had grown so accustomed had become a roiling red sea that foamed and steamed without waves or crests to produce spray. The water writhed against the communications dish a dozen meters away.

"There's not much more we can do here," Luis said. "Leana, get to the center with the others. Tell them to get low and hang on. Paul and I will stay long enough to make sure the machines are acting on their new instructions."

Leana started to object, but steeled herself and nodded. "I love you," she said and ran out the door.

I LOVE YOU TOO, Luis thought.

The building groaned and creaked, then lurched sideways and knocked them off their feet. They were afloat.

Luis jumped up and looked at Paul. "Leana!" he shouted.

"Go!" Paul said, "we've got this!"

Luis bolted through the door and barely kept his feet as the building rocked again. He took several unsteady steps down the hallway.

"Leana!" He called after her.

Behind him, a terrible crash accompanied a metal on metal groan and the distinctive pop of rapid depressurization. The floor pitched as he fought his way back to the Comms room door, where the view through the window nearly paralyzed him.

Inside the room, Paul lay sprawled out on the floor in a puddle of blood that spread outward from his head. Tamra picked herself up and threw herself toward the far wall. She grabbed an emergency kit and pulled out the pressure patch.

Low on the wall, a hole—maybe half a meter in diameter —had been ripped open.

How many times had she trained on a drill just like this?

Tamra moved on pure instinct, with only seconds to act before the pressure and oxygen loss would incapacitate her.

Luis pulled an oxygen mask from a panel in the corridor's opposite wall and put it on. Back at the comms room door, he overrode its emergency seal, braced himself, and hit the button to force it open.

The pressure change stabbed like a knife in his ears, and his whole body burned with pain. It was difficult to see. His eyes, his face, his fingers, his feet, everything felt white hot.

Paul was closest, so Luis grabbed him and dragged him toward the door.

LEANA STRUGGLED to push herself away from the wall. Luis had called her name, then the crash and the deck shoved her into it.

She regained her footing and headed back the way she'd come. She reached the intersection as Luis masked and forced open the door. A pressure wave stabbed her eardrums, but she did her best to ignore it as she ran to the door.

Inside, Luis had wrapped his arms under Paul's and begun to drag him. Tamra lay on the floor near the far wall where Martian daylight shone through a hole.

She grabbed a mask for herself, punched open the door, and rushed in against a wave of searing pain.

"Luis!" she shouted through the mask.

He let her take Paul's left side, and together they dragged him the rest of the way to the door. Luis opened it, and they pulled Paul into the hall.

"Get. Mask." Luis's voice was ragged. He pointed to Paul.

She stepped across the corridor to get a mask, and when she turned back around, Luis was gone. She'd felt the pop of the door opening, but was already in so much pain it had hardly registered.

She masked Paul then returned to the door, where she watched as Luis lifted Tamra, limp, onto his shoulders.

The partially open patch kit lay on the ground near Luis' feet.

Through the hole in the wall, something glinted. The building rocked again under a massive impact, and the wall behind Luis crumpled inward, then was ripped outward by what appeared to be the front-end of a damaged crew transport—afloat and out of control in the seething red foam. Shredded material from the building's skin and internal structures trailed after the transport as it twisted away and pulled a sizeable chunk of the wall and part of the floor with it.

"Luis!" Leana screamed and pounded the window.

Under the influence of Tamra's weight and the building's

motion, Luis lost his balance. He looked for the floor and scrambled to stay on his feet, but only fell back toward the hole.

Leana's throat burned as she reached toward the override button, but the building rocked yet again and she missed, and Tamra and Luis tumbled backward through the mangled wall of the building and into the frigid, boiling water.

Leana screamed.

Luis slipped instantly beneath the surface.

Leana pounded on the window until her screams gave way to rasping sobs. She pounded until other hands restrained her.

LOST

Time was meaningless. Luis was gone, and Leana couldn't cry any more. She stood at the window while, on the other side, the red, indifferent water washed gently into the room. Paul stood behind her and put his hand on her shoulder.

She shrugged it off.

"Leana, I…" he began.

She held up one finger and shook her head. The memory of anger at him buzzed somewhere in her head, but she was numb to it.

"We should go to the others," she said.

"Are you sure?"

"Yes, I'm sure. I can't stand *here* the rest of my life." She recognized a bitterness in her tone that felt disconnected from any feeling. There was a term for this, she knew.

She touched the window and expected cold, but felt nothing. She pushed herself away and started down the corridor. Paul followed.

They found Sheila and several others in an office near the building's center.

"Leana!" Sheila said, "What's happened?"

"What's our status?"

Sheila looked at Paul with a perplexed, concerned expression.

"What's. Our. Status?" Leana repeated.

Sheila snapped her attention back to Leana. "Well, we have four crew transports attached to four HABs and headed toward the rendezvous point. Six of the smaller transports are also underway, towing three other habitats. One of those is the school HAB, and all the kids are accounted for. No injuries. A seventh transport has already reached the rendezvous. We have three people unaccounted for, and two confirmed lost."

"Four."

Again with the look.

"Tamra and… Luis."

"Oh!" Sheila's eyes filled with tears.

Leana looked at Paul. "What about the remotes?"

"Our last readings showed they were moving. We programmed them the best we could to head toward the rendezvous. It's a long shot, but Luis hoped their nav AI would adapt to being waterborne and get them where they need to be. If it doesn't work, we'll have to fish them out ourselves."

"The greenhouse team on shift had four boats prepped and ready to go in the water before we were hit," Leana said, then addressed Sheila directly, "As soon as the boats and the first couple of transports hit the rendezvous point, they should unload and relaunch to help recover the Central Pod. They'll need to get towlines on us and drag us ashore."

Sheila hesitated, and her eyes ping-ponged between Leana and Paul.

"So…" Leana said, "go tell them,"

Leana walked over and grabbed a slate from a nearby table. She touched the patch on her neck and said, "Coordinate and summarize status reports from all colonists and equipment."

She manipulated the slate's interface, and within moments data poured in from the AI's inquiries. The name of every colonist and ID of every piece of autonomous equipment appeared along with their status. Her eyes caught on Michael and Gabriel's names, which were steady green and showed them in the school HAB and en route to the rendezvous under the power of two personal transports. Just above the boys' names, Luis' name flashed red, with the status message *No Response.*

Other names flashed red, but most slowly switched to steady green until only six remained: Luis, Tamra, Deepti, Lucas, Reiner, Mitsuko.

The names burned into her. They seared her in places she would never be able to reach, but none burned deeper or hotter than Luis'. Each red flash of his name hollowed her out until she thought she might collapse in on herself. Her hand touched her belly, and she stared at the slate. The names consumed her.

The Pod lurched under her feet and nearly threw her over. The slate showed that two crew transports had already returned to grapple with the Central Pod. The kids were safely ashore, and the Pod was underway. Soon, she would see them. She would have to tell them. *What do I say? How do you tell your babies their dad is dead?*

They were good, strong boys like their father. They would figure it out. Together.

"GET THOSE SUPPORTS UNDER THERE!" Leana yelled as several colonists, assisted by autonomous rovers, maneuvered temporary support structures into place beneath HAB 7—the tenth they'd recovered.

It was quite a dance to watch. Once automated rovers or

crewed transports beached a HAB, a team of rovers would maneuver under and raise it just enough for two of the larger crew transports to dock on either side. Together, they would slowly trundle up the slope to the colony's new temporary location, where Leana and her team set the supports. Then the transports would return to the water's edge to wait for the next HAB.

Paul and… Luis' efforts to save the colony had mostly paid off. Four of their rovers had adapted to the water well enough to reach the rendezvous point, and they'd brought seven habitats ashore the first day, along with four of the large transports and seven of the smaller ones. The only individual transports they'd recovered had been docked to a HAB or the Central Pod.

There were several casualties—mostly bumps and bruises from the rough ride—but fatalities were mercifully few. Only six had been lost, including Luis.

Only! The pit in Leana's stomach swallowed her til she wanted to puke. *Luis wasn't **only** anything,* she thought, *he was everything.* She clenched her fists until her arms trembled.

Luis and Tamra were the only ones lost to the water, and after a few hours, once the emergency recoveries were done, the smaller transports had triangulated on their sTrans patches and recovered their bodies. Leana could not bring herself to be there when they were brought in—she didn't want to sully her memory of Luis as he had been—vital and alive.

She inspected the habitat's connection to the new supports, then moved on to supervise the next emplacement. Paul—*the goddamned betrayer*—was at the waterline with one of the recovery boat teams.

Leana checked her slate. The AI had captured every project and task she and Paul had set in motion since the transports had gotten grapples on the Central Pod and pulled them to shore. It had taken her two and a half minutes to define the requirements well enough for the AI to build an interface to track and manage all the moving parts of this recovery operation.

All the boats and the four crew transports had returned to the water to recover more HABs, other vehicles, or rovers that had foundered against the crater wall or the rims of smaller craters that lurked like sandbars under the enormous rust-colored lake. For two days they'd worked from sunup til the last tendrils of light sunk below the crater's opposite wall, and had only managed to recover three additional HABs.

It would be close quarters for a while until they'd recovered or rebuilt enough to house everyone comfortably. In the meantime, the Central Pod served double-duty as a temporary shelter.

Things were still in chaos two days post flood, and Leana ached to check another item off her list.

Considerable repair work lay ahead of them. The rising water had churned the abrasive and corrosive martian regolith into a destructive soup. Equipment that managed to survive the flood would have to be thoroughly inspected and cleaned, and the rest salvaged and repurposed, or completely stripped and reconstituted.

If the compositors themselves are even salvageable. The small ones in the Central Pod could only fabricate parts under half a meter. Without the larger ones, now underwater, they wouldn't be able to make larger pieces needed for HAB and equipment repair. Until they could build new compositors, they'd depend on scavenged parts from equipment that was beyond repair.

She'd actively avoided Paul—*asshole!*—since the recovery teams had hauled them ashore. Everything was in shambles, and Luis wasn't here, and Luis had saved *him*. *She* had saved him while Luis was lost to the water. They'd brought him into this project, cajoled him, practically begged him to join them.

And he'd betrayed their trust. He'd betrayed *them*. All over some narcissistic power trip. *How dare he...*

Leana's head swam as Luis' face flashed through her mind, filled with disappointment and anger the night of the election, and then pain, and then falling, falling into rust-colored water.

"Leana!" Paul called over the comms, a note of alarm in his voice.

Where had he come from? *Bastard.* She realized she was on the ground, her hands clutched to her stomach. She struggled back to her feet, her knees still weak. "I'm fine."

"Like hell you're fine. Let's get you back inside."

"I said I'm fine."

"Leana. You need to go inside." He touched her shoulder.

"Get your goddamned hands off me!" Her stomach knotted up again and she swatted his arm away, hard. "These people trusted you! Trusted you!" Leana stood straight, and so close that their helmets clunked together. "*I* trusted you." She narrowed her eyes, her next words nearly growled through clenched teeth. "I know what you did."

Surprise and fear filled Paul's eyes with each syllable she spat.

"I know." She stepped forward and met no resistance as he stepped back. "Luis didn't want to muddy the waters by telling everyone what you did, but you don't give a shit about them, do you? You only care about yourself. You only care as long as you're the one making the decisions."

Step after step, she backed him against the habitat. People nearby watched their silent display, but she didn't care—their proximity meant the comms AI would direct her words only to him unless she requested otherwise.

"I am going to honor the faith Luis' placed in you—despite his damaged trust—as misguided as it may have been. Maybe you can redeem yourself. Maybe you can find that part of you that **he** believed in and earn back my trust—our trust. But you hear me and understand—if you cross the line again, if you abuse your power, or if I even **think** you're serving anything other than the good of this colony, I will expose you and you **will** pay. These people will make you pay. And if they don't, I will."

She turned her back to him and walked to where her slate lay in the martian dust. Before she picked it up, a chime sounded in her helmet.

"Dr. Pendrova, Dr. Robinson? We are…" Tyler began, his voice strung through with excited tension, "we may be getting a transmission. From Earth…"

Leana looked back at Paul, still pressed back against the habitat. "We're on our way to you, Tyler. Out." Leana said both to acknowledge and then cut the transmission.

She strode back over toward Paul.

"Don't ever touch me again," she said. "Ever."

——

CONTACT

——

As Leana and Paul approached the Comms room, her body rebelled. Everything strained under the build up of an energy she couldn't name. Her breath came short and shallow and she tried to get it under control.

They stepped into the room and all she could see was the gaping hole—haphazardly patched—whose ragged outline echoed screams in her head. She stumbled and came up short, as the memory of Luis' fall played through her mind for the thousandth time.

"Leana," Paul approached her but held his hands up in a gesture of surrender. "You don't have to be here. I can take this."

She willed her eyes to focus, to look at him. She willed it, and he would see nothing but pain and anger in them. She didn't respond, but stepped around him and crossed the room to Tyler's station.

"What do you have for us, Tyler?" Leana asked.

"We got a comms ping through the relays. Our system sent out a return ping and alerted me, and I sent a response message. That was… " Tyler checked the time, "thirteen minutes ago. If there's anyone there to receive it, and they replied immediately, I'm expecting a response anytime in the next seven to ten minutes."

"Alright then," she replied, "I guess we just wait."

Leana stepped to the other side of the room and contacted her team to let them know to carry on without her, then returned and took the seat nearest Tyler's console. She turned —in what she hoped was a nonchalant way—away from the patched wall.

They spent the next nine minutes mostly in silence. Paul quietly busied himself at the other comms station, while Leana's efforts **not** to tear into Paul again found her growing increasingly, uncomfortably angry. Tyler managed, with moderate success, to pretend not to notice the tension in the room.

Finally, an audible *ping* from Tyler's console broke the silence, and information played across his screens.

"We're getting something!" he nearly yelped.

Leana swiveled her chair a bit more toward him, and Paul paused his own work and did the same. They all leaned in expectantly.

Momentarily, the screen came to life with a video image of a soldier who quickly introduced himself.

Mars Colony, this is Sergeant Hawthorn of the 675th Mission Support Group supporting the Northern California Emergency Sequestration Facility—an underground government survival shelter. We have around twenty-one hundred inhabitants here, settling in for long-term occupation. We've had intermittent contact with a similar facility near Washington DC.

Leana struggled to reconcile the scope of a twenty-one hundred plus enclave of survivors against the former population of Earth.

The sergeant glanced offscreen and seemed to react to

some kind of signal.

I also have a survivor here, John Hoffstead, with a message for one of the colonists…

Did he just say…

The sergeant stepped out of frame, and before her brain had caught up, there he was.

Hey Leana, it's your dad. I imagine you're pretty surprised to hear from me, and I…

"Dad!" *Holy shit!* "Dad! What!?"

Leana felt lightheaded and reached for the console to steady herself. There he was, on the screen, as words tumbled from his mouth that her brain could not make sense of. Slowly, agonizingly, she caught up to reality. He was alive. And Mel and Danny. Camping? *Of course, camping.*

Tell Luis and the boys I love them too.

His voice rang like a bell in her head, until Luis' name broke her heart in two all over again. A wail escaped from her. A desperate howl at a lost moon.

For him, Luis was still alive. For her, Luis again fell into the ocean of her despair. Leana shook with her sobs—a release she had not allowed herself since the moment itself.

At the edge of her awareness, Tyler and Paul sat quietly, resolutely, almost reverently by. Never in her life had she felt so torn in two. *Drawn and quartered.* She needed her friend, and he was there, only feet away, but he wasn't him anymore, and she couldn't take the emotional overload required to reconcile any of it against what she needed from him. So she hung onto the console and gave herself to the emotional wave. She let it wash over her, to subsume her, and finally to recede.

"I'm sorry," was all she could say for a moment. Then she asked, "Tyler, can you replay that, please?"

Tyler pressed a couple of buttons, and the message jumped back to the beginning.

Mars Colony, this is Sergeant Hawthorn of the 675th Mission Support Group...

The message played back and Leana tried desperately to hold herself together.

...I don't know if you're there to see this or not, but just in case you are... Mel and Danny are here with me, too. We're okay. We were out camping and just happened to be close enough to get the emergency beacon that brought us here. No one here seems to be really sure what's going on, but from what we've been told, it seems no one outside of a place like this could've survived. It looks like we'll be here for a while, though, so we're trying to make the best of it. We've been here since, well, everything happened, and there've been some rough spots, but we're pulling together. I really hope you're alright, and you get this message, and that you and everyone up there are going to be okay. I suppose you're on your own now, so you're probably scrambling to prepare for that just as much as we are here. Hang in there, baby girl, and remember—whatever happens, I love you. Tell Luis and the boys I love them too.

The sergeant stepped back into frame, and signed off with a request for a reply.

"You okay?" Paul asked.

Leana glared at him. "You should reply."

"Sure." Paul looked at Tyler and nodded.

Tyler tapped a couple of buttons on his console. "Ready?"

Paul nodded again and Tyler pressed a final button.

"Sergeant Hawthorn, this is Paul Robinson, Chief Councilor of the Mars colony. We can't express how relieved we are to have received your message. We heard there might be shelters such as yours, but after not hearing anything these first few weeks, and with Earth's satellites revealing nothing, we feared the worst. We've been tracking things there—and tracking the Earth itself as it turns out. We're aware of what happened, but we're still unsure what caused it."

"We are still recovering from recent struggles of our own. The object, whatever it was, has apparently pulled Mars into a tighter orbit around the sun. The planet is warming quickly, and the rising temperatures have melted much of the subsurface and polar water ice, resulting in sudden widespread flooding. We've lost some good people."

Paul looked at his hands in his lap, then back up. "John, I…" He looked at Leana, his face flooded with emotion. He motioned to Tyler to hold the transmission.

Leana moved into view of the camera as Paul moved away. She nodded to Tyler.

"Hey, Dad." She struggled to find some brightness in her tone. "I can't believe it's you! It is so… wonderful to see you!" She felt the abyssal tug of her reality and struggled not to break into tears. "Dad… Dad…" The tears fell. "Luis is gone. The flood." She couldn't look at the camera. Didn't want him to see through whatever facade she managed to project. "There was an accident, and… he's gone."

And with that, she'd told him and her whole body relaxed for what seemed the first time in days.

"Oh, Dad, this was our dream! **Is** our dream." She dried her cheeks. "And we're so close. We *were* so close." Some semblance of composure regained, she looked directly at the camera. "We're still recovering, getting the HABs resettled. The boys are doing okay."

She felt a jolt of unreality from a fundamental thing she'd almost forgotten. "Dad! Oh, my god. Dad, I only just found out! You're about to be a grandpa again! I haven't told **anyone** yet. Luis… Luis didn't even know."

She was only vaguely aware of Paul's reaction in her periphery as he stiffened at this news.

"It's still early, but it's going okay so far, they tell me, but… it's hard. It's so hard without him, Dad." She paused. "Gabriel is so little still. I don't think he understands, but Michael… he's not taking it well. It'll be hardest on him. Maybe soon, maybe you could send him a message? Maybe you could talk to him?"

"Oh, Dad, I can't believe you're alive! It gives me some hope, knowing you're still out there. I love you." She paused again. Looked at Paul. "Okay, I need to give you back to Dr. Robinson." She backed away, then leaned back in. "Oh, and give my love to Mel and Danny, too. We'll talk again soon. Love you."

DISCOVERY

Leana spooned broccoli onto her plate from an open dish. The buffet was no less impressive for her involvement in it. She and a small team had retrieved as much as they could from the partially submerged greenhouse she'd worked so hard to cultivate. The cooks had done a remarkable job putting everything together.

Leana had recommended the banquet to give everyone the chance to recover from the recent tragedy in open company. Though she wanted nothing more than to continue to lose herself in solitary work, to hold tight to Luis' memory—to **not** try to move on, but to feel the keen edge of his loss on her heart—her training blared its alarm bells, and so she'd pushed for this.

Since they'd arrived, the colonists had weathered more hardship and trauma than anyone could have imagined. Only in community would they find peace.

The room was full of people who murmured to each other over their plates. There were a few more lively conversations, but most were reserved. Paul Robinson stood in one corner in animated conversation with a small group.

If they only knew what he'd done.

Despite her anger, the sincerity of Paul's memorial speech had moved her. He had talked about Luis and his sacrifice, and when he did, he'd spoken directly to her, his voice colored by remorse, and his eyes never wavered despite her calculated non-reaction. Were he her patient, she might have judged him reformed and in search of forgiveness, but for now, it took all of her will not to scream obscenities and publicly flay him for his hypocrisies. *Search all you want. I'll never forgive you.*

She turned from the buffet as Gabriel ran past. Laughter trailed behind him and pulled her, momentarily, from the darkness. He was so little, she could hardly expect him to understand what had happened, but Michael understood. Neither had recovered from the shock of the flood before Leana had finally told them. Michael took the news better than she expected. She knew that in some ways it was a put-on—eventually, he would have to confront the loss, and his grief, just like everyone else. But until he was ready, or until he needed her, Leana was content to love him however he needed and to admire his emotional strength.

"Gabriel," she called after her son, "tell your brother it's time to sit and eat." She assumed he heard her, but she wouldn't force the point—they would find her when they were hungry.

She and the boys weren't the only ones with fresh wounds, of course. Three of the colony's children were now orphans, and others—like her boys—had lost a parent. They were young and resilient and would recover relatively quickly, but the scars would follow them forever.

As if those lost to the flood weren't enough, Markus Seiler had left another dark mark on the community a few days earlier when he'd stripped off his helmet and waded into the cold, calm new sea.

A wave of nausea struck—the room felt large and everything far away. Gabriel bounded away in slow motion and his laughter echoed across the vast space between them. She swayed slightly, then reality clamped back down on her like a pressure suit helmet, the murmur of conversation filled her ears, and the scent of the food and the heat of a hundred people washed over her.

Sheila waved to her from a nearby table and indicated a trio of empty seats. A fourth seat stood empty on Sheila's opposite side, and Leana scanned the room again.

Paul was still across the room, mid-schmooze. Her skin crawled and her face flushed. She glanced back at Sheila and recognized the look on her friend's face. *She knew.* Paul had told her. Probably told her what a bitch Leana was, and now Sheila was going to be defensive and hostile. *Damn him! Stupid bastard screwed up everything!*

With just under a hundred people on the entire planet, she and Sheila would have to work it out eventually, and Leana needed a friend now more than ever. She headed for the table.

But it wasn't hostility in her friend's eyes, was it? She wondered as she approached. No, it was more likely the same thing she'd seen from everyone else since the flood… sympathy, compassion, fear, uncertainty, fatigue.

"Sheila," Leana said. It came out colder than she intended.

"Lee," Sheila said. "I… saved some seats for you and the boys."

Leana looked from her friend's pained face to Paul's glowing one, sighed briefly, and sat her plate on the table. She searched the room and found Gabriel and Michael together and headed for the buffet, then took the seat next to Sheila.

For a moment, neither spoke. Under her friend's quiet, sympathetic, protective attention, Leana slowly relaxed. The walk through the room had taken its toll. A week wasn't long enough to deaden the sting of each renewed expression of grief and sympathy. She knew, with her training, who was or wasn't sincere, and while most were, each carefully avoided interaction or veiled comment deepened her wounds. Sheila didn't need to speak—they could read each other well enough without words. They'd both be more prepared to talk about Luis later.

"Paul told me what happened…" Sheila began, "what he did."

"And did he also tell you that Luis should have stopped the election and had them both arrested?" Again, it came out harsher than Leana intended, and she looked away.

"Maybe he should have, but despite how angry he was, he didn't. He had to have had a reason for that," Sheila said. "Paul also told me you threatened everything short of killing him if he got out of line again."

"Hmph."

"He also said you were right." Sheila's eyes were filled with sincerity and sadness. "I hate that Luis was so angry with him when…" Sheila hesitated, "I hate that he had that on his conscience."

"That is something your husband will have to live with," Leana said, "and I hope it tortures him for the rest of his life."

Sheila sucked air, and hurt flooded her face.

Leana almost apologized for the curse, but, like every hour of every day since the flood, Luis fell again into the cold martian sea, and froze the scowl that lingered on her face.

The bastard deserves to be tortured.

TRY AS SHE MIGHT, Leana couldn't ignore Paul any longer. He'd made himself conspicuously inconspicuous as he wandered the outskirts of the room, schmoozed with the colonists, and cast cautious glances their way. Leana knew her expression was anything but welcoming, and she hoped he felt it every time he looked, like a knife in his chest.

Her and Sheila's conversation had retreated to shallower topics after her condemnation of Paul, and for the past five minutes all they'd managed was small talk about the business of the colony.

Paul made his way through the buffet line and entertained the trickle of colonists who approached him until finally he hovered a few tables away, his eyes fixed on Sheila.

In the end, even Leana's obvious animosity couldn't hold him off, and he slunk over and slipped in next to Sheila, muttered a few pleasantries, then tucked into his dinner.

He was uncharacteristically taciturn, but Leana elected to leave it unremarked and to effectively ignore him. Sheila offered her a look that suggested she also noticed, and for a moment neither of them spoke as the tension hung in the air.

It only lasted a moment, though, and soon enough they picked up their conversation as though he wasn't there.

Leana lamented how little sleep she was getting between the morning sickness that forced her out of bed early, and the crazy, hormone fuelled dreams that were waking her up in the middle of the night. As she recounted a recent one about jalapeño and peach jam ice cream covered in extreme amounts of cinnamon powder, Paul snickered.

Leana stiffened as heat rose in her face, but Sheila beat her to a response.

"Something about pregnancy nightmares funny to you?" Sheila asked.

"What?" Paul asked. "No? No. I was... thinking... about the future."

"Right."

"No, I'm serious." He put down his fork and looked from Sheila to Leana.

"Okay. Well, are you going to share?" Sheila asked.

Leana glowered at him, but bit her tongue.

"Okay," Paul began, "so we planned the colony around a genetically viable base population—enough to maintain genetic diversity through the first few generations. However, part of that plan was also for more colonists to follow us and expand that base over time. But now, after all that's happened, it seems we're approaching a point where we may have to, one or two generations down the line, mind you, institute some controls… to catalog and track our genetic diversity, to determine—and enforce—more… genetically advantageous pairings."

Leana's face felt white hot and her scowl deepened, and in her peripheral vision, Sheila's eyes went wide.

Leana struggled to keep her voice down. "So, you think that we need to study, plan, arrange, and track our children's procreation?" She glanced around at the nearby tables, and failed to keep the venom from her tone.

"I think we'll have to consider it, yes." He tried to play it off, but he seemed to shrink ever so slightly under her glare. "But, I'm not about to make some grand decree, if that's what you're worried about." He recovered himself somewhat as he continued. "This is something the community has to choose. Hopefully, everyone will see the logic and participate willingly. If not, then hopefully enough *will* participate that we can maintain a balance. If not, well… it's not really all that funny, but, imagining the sub-human homunculi that would eventually inherit this planet is what made me chuckle."

The cool pinprick of a thought struck her as he spoke, and some of the heat faded as she processed it.

"There is another option," she said.

"I don't think there is. The specialists I've spoken with have all agreed that a strict breeding program is the only way to ensure diversity."

"We have the Cradle."

For a moment, he looked shocked, then understanding brightened his face.

"The Cradle! Of course! Why didn't I remember that?"

Sheila appeared confused, so Leana explained. "It's a seed vault, mostly for our eventual farming and animal husbandry needs. The fact that it also stores human embryos is not common knowledge."

"There are protocols in place," Paul said, "but Luis would have said that it belongs to all of us, and that we don't have to blindly follow protocol, especially now."

Leana cast him a stern, skeptical look, but didn't deny it. Luis would likely have been the first to propose it.

"We'll have to present it to the council," Paul continued, "and let them, and the rest of the colony decide."

For the first time in days, the crushing weight on Leana's heart eased, if only a little.

"I'll put together a team and draw up a proposal for the use of the Cradle," Leana said. "We'll bring it to the council."

"I want my Daddy!"

Michael picked the model rover up off the bed and flung it —in no particular direction. It hit the wall and pieces flew off in different directions. The main drive section clattered to a stop at Gabriel's feet. For a moment, Michael worried a piece might have hit him, and then he wished that one had. He doubled over and screamed, his face buried in the scratchy, rumpled quilt.

"Michael is angry," Gabriel said.

A slight buzz came from Gabriel's direction, and he tilted his head, and listened to the computer. He quietly stepped through the door and into the hallway, and shut the door behind him.

Michael. Nanny used the voice that reminded him of Mommy's bedtime story voice. Somehow, it always made him feel better… eventually.

"Leave me alone."

Michael, Nanny repeated. *What is the matter?*

"I want my Daddy!"

Your father is not here.

"Because he's dead!" Michael sobbed. He tried to hold it back, but he couldn't. He wanted to be strong. He was glad Nanny had told Gabes to go away. He didn't want anyone to see him like this. His chest heaved and his throat burned.

Yes, that is true, Nanny said. *Michael, would you like to see a video of your father?*

"Really? Yes, please."

You may view it on your slate.

Michael picked up the slate from his bedside table and activated the screen.

In the video, Daddy sat at a console in a room that was kind of familiar. He messed with his equipment a little, then looked out of the screen. His face was rounder than Michael remembered, and his skin was darker too, but he looked happy and excited.

Here we go. It's April 13, 2046, at… 7:55pm. Tomorrow's the big day! Lee's giving Michael and Gabriel their baths, and then we're all going to bed early. Big day tomorrow. Big day. I have no idea how any of us will be able to sleep, well, except Gabriel, that boy will sleep no matter what's going on. Michael has been wound up all day. He's big enough to know something's going on, but I don't think he quite understands. He's lived in this house since he was born, except for the month we lived in the simulators before Gabriel came along. He'll turn two a few days before we get there, I just hope he'll be awake for it. We've packed him a tiny birthday cake, with frosting, and candles—the whole works! If we can't do it aboard the ship, we'll just have to do it as soon as we get settled into the HAB. He's such a good boy, and he's already so grown up. He's got this personality that just shines like a beacon. I thought Mars was going to be a great adventure, but this parenting thing… I can't even describe it. Being a dad to these two boys is something else. And now I get to be the first Dad on Mars. He looked off screen, then back again. *Leana needs me. Gotta run. Next video, I'll be floating!*

The screen went dark.

I have six hundred and forty-seven recordings of Luis Pendrova, seventy-eight of which are marked private. Of the remaining videos, four hundred and seventy-two mention you, and you appear in one hundred and thirteen others.

"Can I see the next one?"

The slate's screen lit up again, and there was Daddy floating, holding Michael with a plastic bag up to his mouth.

Michael vaguely remembered the ship and how weird his tummy felt and throwing up—mostly into that bag—while Daddy held him.

Well, Daddy said and smiled. *Here we are.*

"WELL… HERE WE ARE."

Leana leaned back against the wall next to Michael's door, her head light, cold, tight; her eyes swollen with unfallen tears. The lump in her throat nearly choked her and she fought to hold it in—she didn't want to disturb Michael.

She'd come when she heard the crash from Michael's room, but Gabriel came out just as she got there and told her what happened. She listened briefly at the door, then helped Gabriel start his bedtime routine. Then Luis' voice trapped her like a magnet as Michael watched the first video.

She remembered that night. So full of hope, so full of promise. *Fear?* There was fear too, to be sure, but it was wrapped in a rainbow of optimism. They were finally doing it. Finally embarking on their new adventure—together!

The feeling of that night surged in her. The love they shared. The power of the two of them. They could do anything. Together.

Her heart soared with the memory of the feeling, and fell just as quickly into frigid, roiling waters, and she felt compressed to a single point.

How the hell was she supposed to do this without him? To raise two kids—*three kids*. To build a colony. To re-build a civilization? How could she do it on her own?

She listened as Michael watched those early videos. The optimism in Luis' voice was captivating—contagious.

She looked around her. Their little hallway, the living room beyond, the HAB, the colony in its new perch above the waters of Mars.

Gabriel ran out of the bathroom, all smiles. Bouncy. Light. Happy. He jumped into her arms and she held him to her, and he hugged her so hard.

Finally, the tears fell. They streamed down her cheeks as she smiled at their son. She laughed and cried at the same time and squeezed him and pressed her cheek to his.

All of this. All of it was Luis. These boys, this home, this planet. It was everything he'd wanted, and he'd left it here for her.

Together.

—

PROMISE

—

Leana struggled to steer the small boat into the wind. It was inefficient in the choppy water, and their progress was slower than she'd expected.

She hadn't returned to the domed inner crater and its green lake since the flood had driven them onto the parent crater's outer slopes. Others had reported its structure intact, but Leana and her team needed to get inside to confirm its integrity and status. Without the green lake to make oxygen, they would run out in months. It would also take months to build and establish a new agricultural greenhouse to provide food, so they hoped to harvest the lake's algae as a supplemental source of edible bio-matter.

A particularly strong gust seemed to halt their forward momentum, then they lurched forward again. The water was red with martian dust that blew in from outside the crater, and Leana fought against visions of a capsized boat, the two of them dumped into the icy depths. She suggested they hunker down into the boat to reduce their profile against the wind, and it helped, but only a bit. The great dome of the greenhouse rose before them, closer now than the colony on the shore behind.

Alice looked like she was about to be sick in her helmet, and between the wind and the baby's kicks to her stomach, Leana didn't feel so great either.

She gritted her teeth and squeezed her eyes shut to ward off tears as the boat cut through ripples and swells. This filthy red cesspool, locked up for millennia, had risen like a monster to steal her happiness. There was nothing she could do, but she took some satisfaction from the propellers beneath them that sliced through the water and put it to her use.

The crater rim peeked about a meter above the water, and the massive dome loomed over them as they approached.

"Try to find an airlock," Leana instructed.

Alice quickly pointed a few meters ahead to one of the personnel entry platforms that studded the dome's exterior. The stairs that led from the platform to what had been the floor of the main crater now simply disappeared into the water, but would provide a good spot to tie off the boat.

They climbed the stairs and entered the dome through the airlock. Once inside, Leana accessed the nearest console to check system status and sensor readings on the interior atmosphere and the lake itself. The report looked much like it had the last time she'd checked it, only with more green in some places and more red in others.

The numbers matched reports from the colony's monitoring equipment, except that they showed a higher level of particulates from martian soil suspended in the lake water. The particulates should have settled out by now, at least more so than this.

"What do you see?"

"Everything seems normal here," Alice said. "But… well, I can't be sure, but I think there's been some erosion of the inner wall here."

Alice was twenty-five or thirty meters away, and Leana moved to join her. The ruddy bloom in the water seemed consistent with recent erosion, but the bank itself didn't appear to have been disturbed.

"Let's take some samples," Leana said.

She retrieved vials and a long pole from a nearby supply container and gave them to Alice, who used the pole to dip the vials into the lake. Leana capped them and put them in their specimen container.

They walked several meters further on until they reached a break in the walkway where the crater wall had eroded enough that the dome's foundation was exposed. A plume spread out from the spot a few meters into the lake.

"We've seen enough here," Leana said. "We need to get a look at this from the outside."

They returned to the airlock and climbed back down into the boat. Near where they'd found the eroded areas inside, they found that the outer wall was also compromised. Water lapped against the dome's exposed foundation which should have been beneath more than a meter of regolith.

When they were close enough, Leana struggled to see into the shadows inside the crevasse.

"Do you see what I think I see in there?"

"I think so." Alice prepped another set of sample containers.

"I'll get us as close as I can."

She guided the boat within a meter of the eroded section, then gently pushed the prow of the boat into the crater wall. She stabilized the craft as well as she could, while Alice retrieved samples from within and around the fissure.

The samples taken from outside the eroded area showed the same reddish tinge as the rest of the lake, while those from near the exposed foundation were viscous and more greenish-brown than rusty-red.

Alice swished the vials and inspected them. "It's not looking good, Lee."

"Let's get 'em home and see what we've got."

Leana smiled as she pushed the boat back out into the lake and turned it toward the colony. The water was still choppy, but the wind at their backs pushed them faster.

The dome and the green lake were compromised, but that might not necessarily be a bad thing. It seemed the algae had escaped from the lake and been exposed to the Martian environment, and, if Leana's hunch was right, it was flourishing. *That could be a very good thing.*

The colony lay ahead, perched for now on the shore of the new sea. Leana felt the spark of Luis' hopeful optimism and love for this place bloom in her heart. His smile filled her up, and she willed the little boat to go faster. She thought of her boys, the baby that grew inside her, and brown water, blue skies, and the future.

ACKNOWLEDGMENTS

As with most good things in life, writing is hardly a solo endeavor. The creative process needs both time and space, while attention and collaboration are essential to turn creative output into something appealing.

I owe a great deal to my incomparable wife, Sara—my protector of space and time, my encourager, and my first reader. None of this is possible without her support.

Early on in the development of this story—after my initial efforts of "winging it" failed—my friend Nathan helped break the story and nail down the outline that kept me on track while finishing the first draft.

My friend Paul kindly gave me notes on an early draft, and a strong and generous group of readers dug deep into subsequent drafts, providing copious, well-considered notes. Hunter, Nick, Bob, Devon, Garrett, David, Jennifer, and my sister Sara are those valued souls to whom I am extremely grateful. My editor, Alida Winternheimer provided a detailed critique which helped to focus and strengthen the book into what it is today.

In the intervening years, I've been joined on this journey by my honored patrons Cori, Danny B (RIP), Sharon, Chris G, Steven & Ruthie, Dawn, and Chris B., who pledged and provided the support and encouragement I needed to continue to bring this story to life. I am extremely grateful to have such a devoted group of fans, friends, and family.

To all of these people and more who read or expressed interest in my work, I offer my most humble and profound thanks.

ABOUT THE AUTHOR

When I was seven, I wanted to be an astronaut, or, perhaps more accurately, I wanted to be Buck Rogers. At thirteen, I wanted to be a pilot, or, perhaps more accurately, I wanted to be Stringfellow Hawke behind the stick of Airwolf.

Growing up in a small town, where opportunities and aspirations seemed stagnant, even such mundane goals as these—astronaut or pilot—seemed so far out of reach as to be practically unattainable.

Still, their impracticality did nothing to hamper my enjoyment of science, astronomy, or stories about space travel and fantastical adventures. I still wanted to be Captain Kirk, living in an idealistic utopia built on human brotherhood, enabled by scientific advances, and bound by dispassionate but compassionate logic.

As an adult, I've realized how much the stories we enjoy inform and shape our lives, and I've seen how impractical idealism isn't an end unto itself, but it is rather, in the Buddhist vernacular, a finger pointing at the moon.

Story—be it fiction, non-fiction, news and opinion, music, or art—can provide a taste of euphoria, a dose of fear, the thrill of tension, or the pull of love, and can point us toward a better life and a better world, if we only listen.

And that is the goal—to point an idealistic finger toward the moon of a better world. One day I'll get there, and in the meantime, I'll tell the best stories I can, and hope they meet you wherever you find them.

ALSO AVAILABLE

While settlers on Mars fight for their survival, a family on Earth races to escape the rising storms.

Our Once Warm Earth

A *Rogue Planet* novella

A deadly storm.

A beacon of hope.

One peaceful night on the mountain may be humanity's last...

A week after their honeymoon, Mel, her new husband, and her adoptive father are camping on a northern California mountain when a deadly storm rises. A government signal promises protection from the growing global catastrophe that may yet bring the world to its end. Mel must choose whether to stay put and die together or to drag her family through the storm and across the mountain in search of safety.

Learn more here: https://mattr.space/oowe

Our Once Warm Earth and *Inheritance of Dust* are novella-length excerpts from the near-future sci-fi post-apocalypse novel *The Severed Sky* which will soon be recombined and published as a single volume.

THE JOURNEY CONTINUES

If you enjoyed this story, I'd love to share more like it with you.

Follow the ongoing development of the *Rogue Planet* series, keep up-to-date with future stories, go behind-the-scenes, and learn more about me and my writing by joining the crew today.

https://mattr.space/join/iod

As a thank you, I'll send you a link to my Starter Collection which includes two free sci-fi short stories that expand on the world and events of *The Severed Sky*.

For more from *The Severed Sky* right now,

please enjoy the following excerpt.

THE SEVERED SKY

Prologue

21 August 2048
Somewhere above Deadeye Lake
Northern California

The firelight flickered in Melanie's eyes as she lay back against Daniel's chest and looked up at the stars. John remembered long ago when, as newlyweds themselves, he and June had carried on like these two. *Well, not* so *long ago, really. We were always like that.*

They'd been back from their honeymoon for only a week, and still were always together, seemingly always connected. Daniel put his hand on her belly and she moved it down and to the right and held it in place. A moment later she looked up at him and he smiled and kissed her temple.

In the still contentment of the night, John thought about the twists and turns that had brought him and Mel to this point. More than thirty years ago he'd dragged her dad to cover under a hell-storm of bullets and promised to protect and guide her as if she were his own. He'd kept that promise as well as he could and loved her like a daughter through all the hardship and heartache of their lives. He was proud of the woman she'd become.

Not that he didn't still worry about her. She could certainly take care of herself, but he'd worried over her for half his life and could hardly be expected to stop now.

In the months before the wedding, Daniel's work had taken him away from Mel often enough that sometimes it seemed the two spent more time apart than together. When they'd agreed to come up the mountain with him for the weekend, he'd been excited about the chance to spend time with them as a couple. Now here they were, obviously in love and excited to be together. *Maybe I can give up worrying… a little bit.*

The night grew darker and the air cooler, and John stood and stepped closer to the fire. For a moment he enjoyed the heat, then he circled the fire and walked a few paces away. The moon hid behind the mountain, but the fire and the cloudless, star-filled sky gave plenty of light.

The view over the Deadeye Basin and down the western-facing valley had long been one of June's favorites, and it was as beautiful as he remembered. She had found so much joy in this place.

Behind him, the scrape and crunch of rock suggested Mel was up and headed his way. Discretely, he wiped tears from his eyes.

She stepped up behind him, wrapped her arms around his chest, and lay her chin on his shoulder. His eyes welled, and he squeezed her arms around him and pressed his head against hers. They stood like this for several minutes until she let go long enough to step beside him and wrap her arm around his back.

"I'm glad we're here," Mel said. "It's been too long."

"Me too."

"She really loved this place, you know, but not half as much as she loved you."

"I know." Tears fell on John's cheeks and he made no effort to hide them.

"You okay?"

"Yeah," John said. "Gettin' there."

For a moment, they silently took in the view while John scanned the sky, as he did almost every night, to find one tiny light among the thousands. Mars hung just above the valley's southern ridge among a host of stars.

"Where is she tonight?" Mel asked.

John pointed. "Just above the ridge, there."

"Hard to believe she's been up there almost two years already," Mel said. "Building a home and living their dream."

"June was so proud of her," John said. "Me too, once I got past the fact that she was leaving us forever. First, she and Luis haul my only grandkids off to Mars, then Nick moves to Berkley, and now June's gone and it's just me in that big old empty house."

"Well," Mel said, and squeezed him to her side, "my wandering days are over." She patted her belly gently. "Danny and I aren't going anywhere."

"I'll believe that when I see it," John said. "You've never been one to stay put for long."

"I know," Mel said. "I can't explain it, but I'm finally happy. Before things always felt so confined, but with Danny and with the baby on the way, I feel like there are no limits, like the whole world has just been waiting for us."

John smiled and looked down the valley. Under the starlight, the mountain and the forest below it stretched for miles. It had been a long road, and not always an easy one, but he wouldn't trade a moment of it. "It's a very lucky person who finds just what she needs, just when she needs it," he said and kissed her forehead. "I'm happy for you."

"Don't worry too much about Leana," Mel said. "She's exactly where she always wanted to be."

"I'm happy for her, too," John said. "But I miss her and I can't help but worry. She, Luis, and the boys have had the run of the place for two years, I just hope they're really ready for everything to change."

"What are you two conspiring about over there?" Danny called from the other side of the fire. "These marshmallows aren't going to roast themselves!"

Mel ignored him. "I'm sure they'll be fine. Besides, knowing Luis, he's already fermented half the fruit from their greenhouse." She gave John a wink.

A light breeze carried their laughter up the mountain into the dark night.

CONTENT WARNING

Inheritance of Dust contains scenes that may be upsetting to some readers.

Specific content warnings include depictions of natural disaster, personal violence, death, and references to suicide.

In the United States, anyone experiencing a suicidal crisis or emotional distress should call the National Suicide Prevention Lifeline at 1-800-273-8255.